BLOOD MOON CYCLE

BLOOD MOON CYCLE

J.R. SHEPHERD

J.R. Shepherd

Contents

Map

Moon Witch Forest
Terramine
Hortaal
Port City
Sea of Menon
Galbrea
Mercury Mountains
Telatia
Tyr'Anon
Gentry
Serriana
Laytrow
Val'Tora
Serpent's Tongue

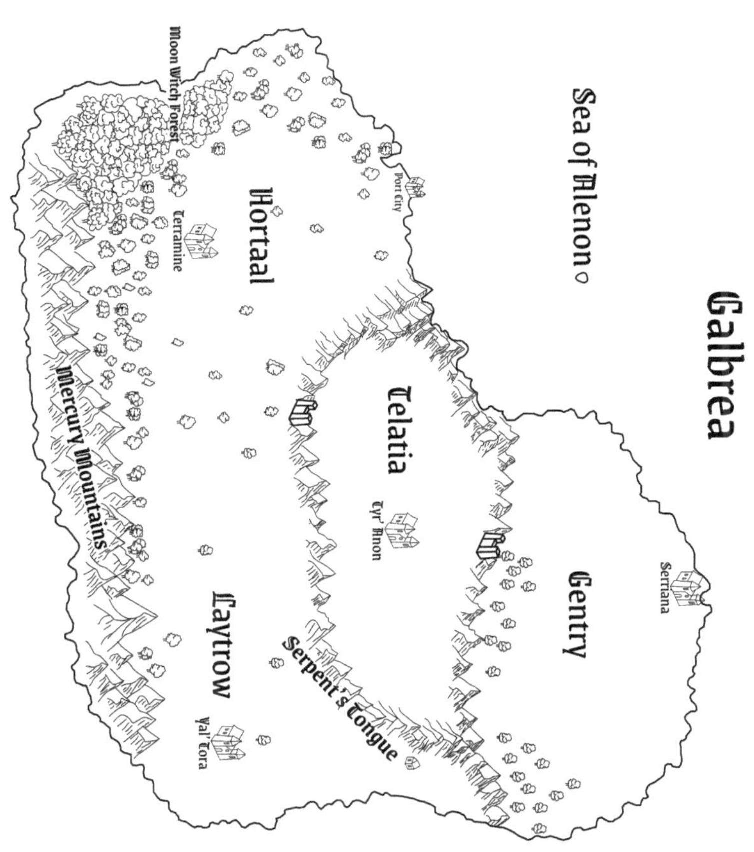

I

Prologue

At the end of an Age, after a thousand years of peace, the middle kingdom of Telatia declared war on all of Galbrea. To answer the call, the three great kingdoms made an alliance. Seafaring Gentry in the north, Laytrow in the southern plains, and forested Hortaal in the west, gathered their armies and assembled themselves at the two Great Gates.

The Great Gates, one in the north and one in the southwest, guarded the only two passes through the Serpent Tongue Mountains which were virtually impassable by man and completely surround Telatia.

Weeks of fighting ensued until the allied kingdoms pushed the Telatian army back into the wastes of Telatia. The allied kingdoms, certain that the Telatians would not give up, posted guards and soldiers at each of the Great Gates. Weeks went by without incident and then the Telatians attacked once again.

This time the Telatian army had received reinforcements

from an unknown source and struck the armies of the allied kingdoms like a violent ocean wave. The allied kingdoms fought valiantly, but began to lose many soldiers and much ground. With the knowledge that they would soon be overrun, and with nowhere else to turn, the allied kingdoms began to search for help. After much thought and study, they chose to search for a legend.

Deep in the Mercury Mountains, a range of mountains in the extreme south of Galbrea in which no man dared venture, was said to live an ageless hermit. The Hermit Mage was said to be one of the only living creatures in all of Galbrea who still remembered the old ways of magic. Hundreds of years before, magic had been considered a dangerous practice only practical in war. The people of Galbrea, fearing that magic would drive the peaceful world back into conflict, held a massive hunt and destroyed all those even thought to have knowledge of the art. Only a few managed to escape. Some into the Mercury Mountains, and some into the deep forests of Hortaal which came to be known as the Moon Witch Forest. Afterwards, magic was lost to Galbrea.

Hoping to appeal to the ageless Hermit, the allied kingdoms sent an ambassador, a young woman named Rielle, into the mountains to seek him out and beg for his aid.

2

Chapter One

Rielle sat huddled by a small fire, her cloak pulled tightly around her.

"I don't see why I had to go on this wild goose chase." She grumbled. "There is no evidence to even support that this Hermit Mage even existed."

"Oh, he exists my lady." Said her guide as he came into the fire's small circle of light carrying an armful of firewood. "People have seen him wandering in these woods at the base of the Mercury Mountains. They say he lives at the top of the highest peak." Rielle scoffed.

"Yes, the conveniently named 'Hermit Peak'. It is utter nonsense." Her guide touched his forehead in a sign to ward off evil.

"I wouldn't speak in such a way my lady. No one knows how forgiving the Hermit Mage might be. I would not wish to have him hear me call him utter nonsense." Rielle waved him off.

"If he even exists, of which I am not yet convinced." Her

guide shrugged and looked around, trying to look into the deep night covering the forest.

"Suit yourself my lady. I was only hired to lead you to the trail that leads to the peak." Rielle shifted into a more comfortable position.

"And how long will that take?" She asked gruffly. The Guide turned back to the fire.

"We will reach the base of the path early tomorrow morning. If you hurried on from there you could reach the peak before nightfall. Or so I hear." Rielle sighed.

"And you cannot be convinced to lead me all the way to the peak?" Her guide shook his head hurriedly.

"No one who enters the Mercury Mountains ever comes back out again. In fact, I would ask you to give up this quest my lady." Rielle glared at the guide.

"I must continue. If we do not do something in the next few months, the Telatians will overcome us. If there is even the slightest chance that this Hermit Mage exists then I must seek him out." She looked back at the fire. "I must." She repeated stubbornly. The guide turned his head ashamedly back towards the woods.

"As you wish my lady." He mumbled. Rielle sat and watched the fire, it's light dancing in her bright blue eyes. She played with her long brown hair for a while and then rolled up in her cloak and went to sleep.

Rielle's guide woke her up early the next morning, just as the sun was rising, and they began what her guide told her would be a 'short hike' to the base of the mountain path. She walked drowsily along behind her guide before she felt a tingle on the back of her neck. She looked around, now fully awake, looking for the cause.

"I think we should move faster." She said. Her guide glanced back at her.

"Why, my lady? We will be there soon and you can get on with your quest." Rielle shook her head.

"No, something is following us, I can feel it." Her tension began to grow.

"Something... following us?" Her guide asked. "Like what? No one, man or beast, would stray this close to the mountains. Nothing in its right mind anyway." Rielle was not comforted.

"No, I am sure something is following us, something malevolent." The guide shook his head.

"My lady, there could not possibly be..." A long, haunting howl filled the air. The guide stopped and turned. "What in the world could that have been?" He asked no one in particular. But Rielle had heard that sound before.

"It is a Felle Wolf. The Telatians use them in battle. That was its Hunting Howl! It's found us!!" She turned and pushed at the guide. "Go! We have to get out of here! The mountains are the only chance we've got." The guide turned aside and let Rielle past him.

"Keep heading south, my lady. The trail starts at a break in the cliffs. You can't miss it." He drew a short cutlass from under his green cloak. Rielle stared at her guide.

"You can't fight this creature. They stand as tall as a man and twice as long, with claws and teeth the length of your sword and twice as sharp." The guide nodded once.

"Maybe so, my lady, but I would rather face this creature than the Mercury Mountains." Rielle shook her head angrily.

"Then you will die a fool." Another howl filled the air. Rielle growled at herself and then turned and began to run. She ran gracefully between the small trees until they began to thin out. Then a blood curdling scream filled the cool morning air, accompanied by a howl and a gurgle as the scream was cut off. Rielle shivered and ran faster.

In a matter of moments she found herself at a cliff wall. She stopped and glanced frantically back and forth.

"Keep going south, the trail starts at a break in the cliffs. You can't miss it." She repeated to herself. "But which way along the cliffs? Fool of a man, he should have just ran. Then I wouldn't be in this position." She heard the Felle Wolf howl again. Rielle began to panic. "Which way!?" She yelled at the cliff. Almost immediately, She heard an echo to her left. "East." She whispered. "It must be east." She turned to her left and started running again.

After a few seconds she entered a clearing and along the cliffs she saw a narrow opening. Rielle nearly cried with relief and was halfway across the clearing when she felt the back of her neck tingle again. She couldn't help herself, she slowed and came to a stop. Then, slowly, she turned around and stared into the forest.

Two midnight blue eyes stared back at her. Immediately Rielle knew she should not have stopped. No matter how hard she tried, she could not will herself to move. The Felle Wolf stepped out into the clearing and looked at its new prey. It was even bigger than the ones she had seen at the Great

South-Western Gate when they had attacked at the beginning of the second wave.

Rielle began to shake fearfully and the wolf turned its head to one side. 'It's amused' She thought to herself. 'It likes seeing me afraid.' Rage boiled up inside her and replaced the fear. She forced herself to stop shaking and shook her head to clear it.

"I may not be capable of defending myself against you." She told the wolf. Then she lifted her head pridefully and stamped her foot. "But, I'm not going to let you eat me without a fight." The wolf crouched down and let out a low, menacing growl. Rielle felt fear creeping back into her again.

"Well run you silly girl!" Came a voice from behind Rielle. Rielle looked back and saw a man in a dark cloak, holding a bow, standing near the opening in the cliffs. Shocked into action, Rielle took off at a dead run. The wolf howled behind her and Rielle faltered.

"Don't stop girl, Run!" For some reason the man's voice held more sway to Rielle than the Wolf's terrifying howl and she continued to run. She heard a stick snap behind her as the wolf leapt forward to give chase. Then an arrow hissed past Rielle's left ear. She flinched and slowed again, then jumped and kept running when she heard the man yell. Another arrow, and this time a pained yelp followed.

Two more arrows in quick succession and Rielle heard a heavy thud behind her. She ran a few more steps and into the opening in the cliff. She sat there with her back to the wall for a moment, and then peeked out. Rielle gasped.

Only a few yards behind where she had been when the last two arrows flew past her head, lay the wolf, breathing heavily on the ground, dark blood oozing from the four expertly placed arrows.

The man calmly walked across the open ground and knelt down beside the wolf. Rielle heard a low growl, but the wolf seemed to be too weak to attack. The man stayed beside the wolf for a moment then, in a lightning quick movement, drew a long curved sword from beneath his cloak and plunged it into the wolf's chest. The wolf jerked and then laid perfectly still. The man withdrew his sword, swung it once to remove the blood from the blade, then returned it to its scabbard beneath his cloak.

Rielle slipped back behind the cliff wall, hoping the man would leave and forget about her. She waited silently for a few moments and then relaxed.

"I think he is gone." She told herself aloud.

"Who is gone?" Asked a voice beside her. Rielle squealed and jumped back out into the clearing, promptly falling over backwards. Rielle looked up as the man came out of the mountain path, frantically looking back and forth.

"It's not another Wolf is it?" Rielle looked at him in surprise.

"No, you startled me." The man looked down at himself.

"Me? How could I startle someone like you? Silly girl." Rielle scowled.

"Silly girl?" The man shrugged and offered his hand to her.

"How else do you describe someone with no weapons, standing stalk still in the open, and yelling at a Felle Wolf that they aren't going to let it eat them?" He asked as he pulled Rielle to her feet. She opened her mouth to speak and then closed it again. She thought for a moment then scowled again.

"Well what do you call it when you go around shooting arrows inches away from my head? You could have killed me!" The man shrugged again.

"I call it saving your life." Rielle opened her mouth, but again could find nothing to say and closed it. "Speaking of silly." The man said, turning and looking at the mountain path. "Who would actually want to go into the Mercury Mountains anyway?" Rielle spoke up, glad to have something to say.

"We are going to the Hermit Peak to look for the Hermit Mage, if he exists."

"We?" The man asked, looking back around at Rielle. Rielle nodded.

"Yes, Me and my...my..." She stopped, thinking back on what had happened.

"Your guide?" The man asked. Rielle nodded.

"Yes, my guide. I didn't even know his name."

"Lyng-rin. That was his name." The man said, unstringing his bow and placing it in a long leather tube.

"Lyng-rin?" Rielle asked. The man nodded.

"Yes, he grew up in a village not far from here. Unfortunately I was not able to get here in time to save him as well." The man slung his, now packed, bow over his shoulder. "I suppose you will need a new guide then." Rielle looked back at the man. She suddenly realized that he had had his hood up the whole time and she had not seen his face.

"I suppose... but... what about Lyng-rin?" The man turned and started towards the opening in the cliff.

"The locals leave the bodies of the dead in the forest to be taken by the earth. He has already been given as good a burial as any he would have received." Rielle tilted her head and thought for a moment and then realized she was being left behind.

"Wait, does this mean you will guide me up the mountain?" The man shrugged again, a habit he seemed to have, Rielle noticed.

"I suppose no one else is around to do it, so that leaves me."

"But I don't even know who you are, or what you even look like for that matter." The man stopped in the trail and Rielle almost ran into his back in her hurry to catch up.

"I suppose not." The man turned and pulled back his hood. Rielle almost gasped. He seemed to be a young man, but his head was covered in silver white hair that reached his shoulders, some in thin elegant braids. He had liquid blue eyes and a bright smile. He held his hand out to Rielle, careful to keep his eyes averted.

"I am Solidus." Rielle cautiously took his hand and shook it.

"I'm Rielle." He nodded and then turned back to the trail.

"Shall we move on then Rielle?" Rielle nodded and followed him up into the mountains.

"Why are you willing to lead me up here? No one else seems to be willing to even go near the mountains at all." Solidus chuckled.

"I have lived near these mountains for a long time and I know how to handle myself around them. Besides, anyone not afraid of the mountains is either very brave, very powerful, or very foolish. But I can't let such a silly girl be more brave than me now can I?"

"Or more foolish." Rielle countered. Solidus chuckled again.

"Perhaps."

Chapter Two

Rielle sat huddled in a cave beside a small fire Solidus had managed to build. Outside, the wind howled and stinging snow filled the air. Solidus stood near the entrance looking out.

"It should soon slow down enough to make it to the summit. There was a cabin built there a long time ago and should provide much better shelter." Rielle nodded and pulled her cloak tighter around her.

"You know," Solidus said, without turning around. "You will stay warmer if you don't bundle up so tightly." Rielle glanced up.

"What?" She asked quizzically. Solidus turned and made his way back to the fire and threw a few more sticks onto the tiny blaze.

"If you bundle your cloak around you tightly, then the air cools your cloak and your cloak cools you. If you let it stay out from you, then you warm the air and the air acts as a buffer between you and the cold cloak. Then the cloak holds in the warm air and keeps you warm." To demonstrate, Solidus sat on the cave floor close to the fire and set his cloak over himself like a tent. Then he opened the front of his cloak to let in what little heat the fire could provide. It had been hard to follow what he had said, but Rielle copied him and when she opened her cloak she felt herself warm slightly.

"Amazing." She said. Solidus shook his head.

"No, what is amazing is how many people freeze at night because they think bundling up makes them warmer. Then they wonder why they were cold all night." He chuckled to himself. "People amaze me." Rielle laughed a little.

"Not everyone is that bad just because of that one point." Solidus nodded.

"True, but you mistake me. People amaze me. Not only in how naïve they can be, but also in how skilled they can be, how intuitive they can be, and how creative they can be. The human being can be an amazing creature. Then again, they can also be horrible, vicious, prideful, greedy, violent things. And worst, they never learn from their own mistakes." Rielle looked at Solidus.

"Of course they do. Without learning from our mistakes we would never advance." Solidus half smiled.

"And yet, no matter how far humans advance, they forever repeat the mistakes of the past. Even before the thousand years of peace there were wars, and contentions, and struggles for power. And though the loss of human life was great and peace ensued from remembering the pains of those struggles, you always manage to start another war and more lives are lost." Solidus stared into the flames, which had seemed to burn brighter as he spoke. Rielle thought silently for a moment.

"Wait, you said, You always manage to start another war. You said, Humans do not learn from their mistakes. As if you were not part of the human race." She stared at him hard. Solidus half smiled and chuckled to himself.

"It seems I have been away from people too long and have let my tongue slip away in my frustration. You are a bright young woman to have caught it." Rielle stared for a moment longer and then understanding dawned on her.

"The Hermit Mage." She whispered. Solidus locked eyes with her, the blue color draining from them and leaving them a clear silver. She immediately saw why he had never made eye contact with her before. Through his eyes, Rielle could see limitless knowledge and power, and a cool agelessness that made him seem far older than he appeared. Solidus half bowed from his position on the floor, never breaking eye contact.

"Grandmaster Silver Mage Solidus, Or as I am more commonly known, The Ageless Hermit Mage. At your service" Rielle sat in shock for a few moments.

'I have been searching for the Hermit Mage, and all this time he has been my guide? It can't be, it just can't be. It is too convenient.' She looked back at Solidus.

"How can you possibly be the Hermit mage? How do I know you aren't trying to trick me in some way?" Solidus laughed.

"I suppose there is really no way I can definitively prove it to you, young Rielle Toriel Lyvinius of Hortaal." Solidus reached into the fire and pulled out a small handful of flames.

He let the flames dance in the palm of his hand for a moment then forced them into a small orb which he then, like liquid, poured back onto the fire, Rielle watching in astonishment all the while.

"I guess you will just have to take my word for it." Rielle sat silently, staring intently at Solidus. Now, he fearlessly met her gaze.

'It just cannot be. The Hermit Mage was a myth, a legend. He can't exist. But the fire... and that ageless look in his eyes, how could he be anyone else?' Rielle's lip began to tremble. She slid back on her knees and bowed low to the ground, her arms stretched before her.

"Please, Great Mage Solidus, you must help..."

"The allied kingdoms in their hour of need before they are overrun by the forces of the Telatian army and their unknown reinforcements. Yes, I know." Despite herself, Rielle felt angry with Solidus for interrupting her prepared statement. Solidus stood and, with a wave of his hand, extinguished the fire.

"The storm has abated, we may discuss this matter at my home on the peak. We are not far from it now." Rielle looked outside the cave to see that the storm had, indeed, stopped and afternoon sunlight was beginning to break through the clouds. She stood shakily and brushed off her knees and followed Solidus from the cave onto the mountain path. Following quietly behind Solidus, Rielle carefully planned how best to convince him to help.

* * *

"No!? What do you mean, No!?" Rielle exclaimed. Solidus sat at a small table and flinched as Rielle yelled.

"I cannot help you. I won't shed blood unless it is absolutely necessary. And before you say it, your war is not a necessity." Rielle scowled.

"How is war not a necessity?" Solidus sighed.

"It is hard for me to explain, but this war may still be averted. There are choices that may still be made that can turn it aside. When those choices are made it will create other choices that could also change the outcome of the war. If those choices are made, and the full war begins, then, perhaps, I may help. But only then, and only if I choose to."

"We are already at war!" Rielle yelled, causing Solidus to flinch again. "It can't be turned back, we are already fighting, and Losing!" Solidus shook his head sadly.

"You could not possibly comprehend what this small battle could become. It is only a precursor to a much greater catastrophe, that can be avoided if the right decisions are made. If not, then you will have much greater worries than holding a few insignificant gates against human enemies." Rielle faltered.

"Worse than the tragedies already taking place? It couldn't be." Solidus sighed.

"In this age of peace you have forgotten what war can truly become. Very well. If you want my help that much, then I will teach you and you can support the allied kingdoms yourself." Rielle halted completely.

"What did you say?" She asked, confusion coloring her voice.

"I will teach you what you wish to gain from me and you can support the kingdoms." Rielle shook her head emphatically.

"No, I couldn't possibly do magic. Not at all." Solidus stood.

"You have strong mage potential, you descend from the old lines of Hortaal. Not the kingdom itself, but the one for whom the kingdom is named. One of the greatest masters of all time, Lotus Grandmaster Hortaal Lyvinius, my first and most talented student." Rielle's jaw dropped.

"You taught High King Hortaal? That isn't possible you would have to be... well... old." Solidus chuckled.

"They don't call me ageless because I don't have wrinkles." Rielle stared at Solidus.

"Be that as it may, I can't possibly have mage potential. I would know if I did." Solidus shook his head.

"Many people have the mage potential, but almost no one discovers it on their own. It takes skill and training to bring it out. Some have it come to them naturally, but only a very few. And in these days, when magic has been banished from the world, it has become nearly impossible for one to know their potential." Rielle was not convinced.

"I still don't believe I am a mage." Solidus nodded and stood from the table.

"Of course you don't. You have been taught from a young age that magic is a terrible thing. Why, now, would you turn and embrace it?" Solidus took a small clay mug from a shelf and went outside and filled it with freshly fallen snow. Bringing it back inside, he handed the mug to Rielle.

"Hold this please." Rielle took the mug and held it between her two hands. "Would you mind taking a quick test? If I am wrong nothing will happen and we have lost only a small amount of time. If I am right then you will realize your potential for being a mage. Is this acceptable?" Rielle harrumphed.

"I suppose it wouldn't hurt to try." Solidus nodded and began rummaging around through containers and cupboards.

"First, we have a cup of tea. Then we shall see your potential." Rielle followed Solidus with her eyes.

"How will you heat the water? I don't see a cooking fire." Solidus chuckled.

"A little thought will solve the problem." Rielle looked at him with one eyebrow raised.

"Thought? About what?" Solidus grunted in triumph.

"Aha! I found the tea. As for thought, young Rielle, the thoughts are Fire."

"Fire?" She questioned.

"Heat, Combustion."

"What are you talking about?" Solidus turned and walked slowly towards Rielle. "Passion, intensity, inferno, power, warmth, blaze, Fire." Solidus stepped within inches of Rielle. After a moment of hard staring Rielle felt her cheeks burning and Solidus smiled.

"And thus these thoughts bring us our solution." Rielle drew breath to voice her confusion and felt warm steam fill her lungs.

'*Steam?*' Rielle looked down at her hands. The mug sat there, still clutched tightly in her hands, but the snow inside had melted away and the water inside steamed as if it were about to boil. Rielle stared at the mug as Solidus took it away from her and prepared two cups of tea, pouring the steaming water over the leaves. Solidus took a sip and sighed.

"You make excellent tea Rielle, why not try some?" He

pushed the second cup of tea across the table and sat in his chair. Rielle sat at the table and took a sip of the tea Solidus had placed in front of her. It tasted excellent, and was at the perfect temperature for drinking. Solidus sat grinning and sipping at his tea. Rielle stared into her cup.

"How did the snow melt so quickly." She looked up at Solidus. "Did you...?" Solidus shook his head.

"No, it was all you. I only provided the thoughts you needed. With your hands close together your energy flows naturally. Then the thoughts of heat and warmth caused you to heat the mug with your inner power. You have mage potential." Rielle sat silently in her chair, staring blankly at the tabletop. Solidus finished his tea and set the cup on the table.

"Do you know how to meditate?" Rielle jumped slightly, being shocked back into conscious thought again.

"Um, yes. As an ambassador, I was trained in many forms of meditation to help keep calm and thoughtful during difficult discussions." Solidus nodded.

"Good, come with me." Rielle stood shakily and followed Solidus into a tiny room built into the side of the small cottage. Inside, Solidus waved his hand through the air and hundreds of candles lit, covering every inch of the walls and floor except one small space in its center. Solidus beckoned Rielle into the room and had her sit in the center of the floor.

"Sit here and meditate. Come to terms with what you are and accept it. When you have cast aside all of the things you have been taught about magic up to this point. When you have come to fully accept it as not just a weapon of war, but as a tool to create, a skill to heal, and, of its self, an art... then come to me and we will begin to teach you to use the great gift you have been given." Solidus turned and closed the door behind him, leaving Rielle with nothing but the candles to keep her company.

Rielle watched him go, then glanced around at the hundreds of flickering candles. Taking a shuddering breath, she sat quietly and struggled to slow her rapid heartbeat with slow measured breaths. For what seemed like hours she sat and contemplated the mug of snow, trying to think of any other explanation for what had happened. Eventually she had to accept that there was no other explanation than the answer Solidus had given her.

She realized that she had been taught to fear magic as a dark and demonic power that warped it's wielders into frenzied psychopaths. And events in her past had led her to accept that as truth. But now that she had met the Hermit Mage Solidus, and somehow used that power herself, she found that what she had been taught could not be the entire truth. At the very least what she had done had not Felt like Dark sorcery.

The time drifted away as she struggled to accept that she had gone out to search for help, but would return as the help she had been sent to find. Rielle's stomach growled as the scent of food drifted into the room where she was meditating. After a few moments of struggle between mind and stomach, stomach finally won and Rielle stood and left the room.

She found Solidus hard at work in front of a small stone oven, chopping vegetables and stirring something in the oven periodically.

"I thought you might be coming out soon." Solidus commented, tossing a handful of something into whatever was in the oven. "Supper is almost ready. There are some bowls and plates in a cupboard just over there." He waved vaguely behind him without turning around. "If you wouldn't mind, it would be helpful if you would set the table."

Rielle looked around and made her way to the cupboards and began searching for the bowls. When she had found the dishes, she made her way back to the table and placed them across from each other and then turned and watched Solidus pull a steaming pot of stew from the oven.

He made his way to the table and sat it in the center and then returned to the oven. After a few moments he reached in and pulled out a juicy roast which he also placed on the table.

He shuffled through a few drawers and cupboards before returning with forks and knives. Placing them on the table, Solidus slid out a chair and motioned for Rielle to sit. He slid the chair forward as she sat and then took his own seat. Rielle watched Solidus as he carved the roast and placed the first piece on her plate. Solidus half smiled, seeming to read her mind.

"My manners surprise you? I may be a hermit, but I was not always shunned by civilization. You seem to forget that I taught High King Hortaal and some few others, and I was a high standing member of society. That may be why your superiors were able to find records of me. An oversight for which I blame myself." Rielle could not respond. She had never before met anyone who could read her so easily as the seemingly young man across from her. Solidus chuckled.

"When you have been around as long as I have, you tend to pick up on certain things." Rielle blushed and resolved to not be so openly readable. Solidus smiled knowingly, but said nothing. She sampled each bit of food and marveled at the harmony of flavors that filled her senses. After eating her fill, Rielle wiped her mouth lightly with a handkerchief.

"That was a very good meal." She stated as Solidus cleaned off the table and placed the empty dishes in a wash basin. Solidus nodded.

"Thank you. I have been practicing for a very long time." He held his hand over the wash basin and made a quick, smooth movement. The basin filled with steaming water and Solidus added some soap before reaching in and scrubbing the dishes clean. Rielle watched him for a few moments.

"Why do you not use magic for that? You filled the basin with water and heated it with magic, yet you clean the dishes by hand." Solidus half smiled.

"Magic is mechanical. Working with your hands has meaning." He stated. Rielle tilted her head, uncomprehending. Solidus scratched his chin, searching for the proper words and leaving a slight film of soap on his face.

"Let me put it another way. Being an ambassador, you know how to argue a point, correct?" Rielle nodded and Solidus returned the gesture. "Imagine that every argument could be won by a simple, preconceived statement. That is like magic. Though it may be faster, and easier, it means nothing. It does not show what you can or cannot do. It does not have any meaning for anyone involved. It is mechanical. But if you get down and use your hands or, in your case, use your intellect to convince another party of your point, then it has become something that you can have pride in and grow from." Solidus turned back to his dishes and continued scrubbing to let Rielle absorb what he had said.

Rielle slowly understood what Solidus meant and then sat back at the table and stared at the floor. Solidus finished his work and turned, grabbing a towel to dry his hands as the dishes put themselves away.

"What holds your thoughts now?" Solidus asked her. Rielle looked up at his calm face, staring into his bottomless eyes.

"How can I learn magic? There are so many things I feel I am supposed to know before I could use it. How do I know what I am supposed to think?" Solidus smiled and laid the towel aside and sat at the table across from Rielle.

"Magic is a simple art. What I have said thus far have not been rules of magic itself. It is a philosophy that I encourage all of my students to embrace. If you can do it with your own two hands I encourage you to do so. Doing everything with magic could cause you to become callous and unfeeling. Being entirely dependent on your magic causes you to have fatal weaknesses in other areas. Even the greatest mage in the universe could not survive a knife to the heart. But a well trained warrior can sense the attack and deflect it without thought." Rielle listened carefully.

"So, if you develop other skills, then, in a tense situation, they could protect you long enough to do what is necessary." Solidus nodded.

"Exactly, an action that you have practiced over and over again will aid you more precisely and more quickly than if you have to gather your will to use magic." Rielle nodded and then frowned.

"But what if you get into a situation in which you have no experience?" Solidus nodded seriously.

"That is a good question to ask and leads us to your first

lesson." Solidus stood and Rielle quickly followed. She followed him from the small cabin and out onto a bare space of rock just outside. The wind blew across the peak and chilled Rielle through her cloak. She pulled it around her and looked out over the clear sky. Mountain peaks rose up around them like jagged claws reaching to tear at the sky. Far to the north she could see the vast plains of Laytrow stretching out into the horizon. They seemed small to Rielle from her vantage point on the peak.

"Very rarely do the clouds clear from the peaks enough to see the view." Rielle was shook out of her daydream by Solidus's voice. "You asked a question." He continued. "Would you like an answer?" Rielle turned herself towards Solidus and nodded.

"Yes." She said simply. Solidus returned the nod.

"When in a situation that you have no experience, you must first assess the situation. If you are not in danger, then you have time to think through the problem and find a solution. If you are in harm's way, then you must protect yourself accordingly."

"What do you mean?" Rielle asked. Solidus smiled at her continuing questions.

"There are two main kinds of danger, Magical and Physical. Magical danger could be another mage attacking you with their magic, or something could be trying to invade your mind. Physical danger could be a knife in the dark or a mountain falling on your head." Rielle swallowed hard.

"How do you protect yourself from something like that?" She asked. Solidus raised his hands in front of him, his left hand resting under his right arm.

"You create a barrier between yourself and the danger." To demonstrate, Solidus fluidly moved his hands across his body and shifted his feet into a wider stance. A shimmering barrier of silver energy accumulated around him into a small dome.

"There are two types of barriers." Solidus said from inside his dome of energy. "Shields, which protect you from physical danger, and Wards, which protect you from magical and mental attacks. Each are almost useless against the other." Rielle stared on.

"So a Ward will protect you from magic but not physical attacks?" Solidus nodded and let his barrier melt away.

"Exactly. Now you try and make a Shield around yourself." Rielle glanced at her hands.

"How?" Solidus smiled patiently.

"To protect yourself from something, you must understand the nature of it. Physical harm is easy to understand. A knife or sword can cut, a club can bludgeon, but for these things to do so they must reach your body. You create your shield with your inner power to keep these physical forces away from you. First, you must feel your energy flowing through you." Rielle looked a little lost. Solidus motioned towards her. "Close your eyes." She did as he asked.

"Breath deeply and slowly. Feel each breath enter your body and each exhale leave your body." Rielle focused on the air filling and then leaving her lungs. Solidus continued. "As you breath, feel your heart beating, making harmony with each breath. As your heart beats, feel the blood rush through you to each part of your body." Solidus paused until he could see that Rielle was following him. "Now that you can feel everything you are doing... ignore it." Rielle opened her eyes.

"Ignore my heart and my breathing?" Solidus nodded.

"These things have been happening from the moment of your birth. You should not have to think about them. Let them continue on without your mind attached to them." Rielle nodded and closed her eyes again. She tried and tried but her thoughts always seemed to return to how she was breathing. Solidus seemed to see her struggle.

"Let your mind wander. Let it latch on to anything it can find to steer your thoughts away from your breathing." Immediately her mind latched onto Solidus. She didn't understand why, but she could suddenly visualize him standing before her with a patient smile.

"Good." He told her. "Now that you can see with your mind, stretch it out to see beyond just me." Rielle blushed slightly and lost her vision for a moment. Slowly, she rebuilt it, taking in Solidus, the bare ground around them, and the small hut. "Good." Solidus repeated. "Now, continue to ignore your breathing and your heart, but turn your attention back inward, on your own body." Rielle did as she was asked and, for a moment, her attention went back to her breathing. But, after a few moments of silence, Rielle suddenly felt a pulse. It started in her abdomen, flowed through her entire body, and returned to its point of origin. After a few seconds she felt it again, a pulse of energy flowing through her.

"Excellent." Solidus said. Rielle opened her eyes.

"That is incredible." She whispered. Solidus nodded.

"That is the origin of your inner power. It starts in your core and flows throughout your body much like your heart pumps blood. But, unlike your heart, you can influence your inner power. You can will it to beat faster, to increase the power flowing through you, or you can make it beat slower, to hide it. When you make your shield I want you to will your power to beat faster, then lead it through your body to your arms and down to your hands. Once there, let it build until you don't think you can hold it any longer." Rielle nodded and closed her eyes and felt for the pulse again. Once she found it she counted each pulse in her mind.

Then, not really understanding how, she willed it to go faster. First one beat, and then another pushed flowing tides of warmth throughout Rielle's body. She struggled to get hold of the energy but was unable to direct it to her arms. She heard Solidus speak again.

"Start by thinking of your energy as a river. It flows down many channels and not always where you want it to go. Shut off each branch as it comes to it and direct it down the stream you want." Rielle concentrated on the energy flowing down into her legs and imagined a door closing the power off from its stream. Immediately her legs felt cold and she felt tension grow in her arms and chest. After a few tries, Rielle created a wall instead of a door, starting at her waist. Then she imagined the wall pushing upward, forcing the energy up into her shoulders. When the wall reached her shoulders, she felt the energy flow down her arms and into her clenched hands. Solidus spoke once again.

"As your energy builds stand straight and tall, as if in the presence of royalty." Rielle corrected her bent over posture. "Now keep your elbows at your side and lift your hands in front of you. Imagine a dome forming around you. A dome of energy, flowing like water, denying passage to anything from the physical world." Rielle obeyed the command and built the image in her mind. By the time she had finished she felt as if her arms were burning and she ached to let go of the bottled up energy inside her. Solidus let her struggle with herself for a few seconds before giving a final instruction.

"Now, open your hands slowly and let the energy inside you fill the image of the shield around you." Rielle gratefully opened her hands and felt the power she had built rush out of her. She willed it to fill what she had imagined her shield should be and felt a slight pressure over her whole body.

"Open your eyes." She heard Solidus say. Slowly she opened her eyes and light filled her vision. Around her was a smooth purple dome of flowing energy. Through it, she could see Solidus standing at the other side of the small clearing, a smile on his face.

"I did it." Rielle muttered to herself and she saw Solidus nod.

"You did very well for your first time. With practice you will be able to build the energy, and create the shield, in an instant." Rielle looked around her.

"I feel pressure." She said. Solidus nodded.

"It is your personal map to your shield. You will be able to feel where your shield is weak, or from where an attack is coming." To demonstrate, Solidus picked up a small stone and threw it at Rielle. It struck the shield in front of her face and bounced off, landing harmlessly on the ground. As the stone hit, Rielle felt a slight pressure on the tip of her nose that left it tingling.

"The added pressure you felt was your shield deflecting the stone. In this way you can tell from where your enemy is attacking and can add power to that place to strengthen it."

Rielle nodded her understanding and Solidus nodded again in return.

"Good. Now, bring your hands down to your sides and imagine the dome around you draining away. Then open all the barriers you placed inside yourself and let your power flow freely again." Rielle dropped her hands to her side and felt the pressure from her shield drain away from head to toe. She removed the wall and opened the doors in her body and felt her energy pulse through her like it had before. Instantly she felt weak and nearly dropped to her knees.

"You will get used to the drain. Your body will recover in a few minutes and you will feel the same as always." Rielle looked up at Solidus and opened her mouth to speak but saw a strange expression enter his features. Like a bolt of lightning, Solidus drew his sword from beneath his robe and rushed at Rielle. Unable to move in her weakened state, Rielle squeezed her eyes shut and gasped as she felt Solidus's sword pass beneath her right arm. She could feel Solidus breathing in measured breaths by her left ear.

"Run." He whispered. "Ignore the weakness and run." Without understanding why, Rielle ducked and ran towards the cabin. When she reached the door, panting heavily, she turned and looked at Solidus. The Hermit Mage stood over a figure in black clothing, wiping his sword clean.

"Go inside, Rielle. You will be safe there." He called. Rielle saw another black clad figure with a mask come up the path to the cabin and ran inside, bolting the door behind her. She ran to a window and gazed out. The black clad figure slowly circled Solidus, a long curved dagger in his hand. Solidus looked on calmly, his sword hanging loosely in one hand.

When the figure struck, Rielle could hardly keep track of what happened. One instant the figure had launched themselves at Solidus, dagger held to strike. And the next instant, Solidus had moved out of the way and struck a fatal blow with his sword. The figure crumpled and laid unmoving.

Another two figures came up the path and another leapt from the roof of the cabin in front of Rielle, causing her to scream. The figure spared only a glance towards her and then moved to join it's comrades in a circle around Solidus. They circled for a few moments and then Rielle heard Solidus speak.

"You don't have to do this you know." He told the figures. "You still have the chance of taking your dead and leaving this place alive." The figures continued to circle. "It is bad enough that you were forced to come to these mountains in the first place. You have shown great strength of heart just by coming here." One of the figures faltered for half a step and then continued to circle. Solidus noticed and glanced at the figure.

"I know you don't want to be here, why not return to your families? I have given all the warning I can give. If you continue this nonsense there will be more pointless bloodshed." The figure faltered again, but this time the other two jumped in to attack. Rielle watched in awe as Solidus masterfully deflected one figure and killed the second in one movement. He turned and disarmed the third figure, twisting in time to deflect the first figure a second time. With a swing of his sword, Solidus crippled the third figure then twisted it behind him and the first figure ran onto the blade. With a gurgle, the first figure went down and Solidus swung his sword to remove the blood.

Rielle, finding strength to move, opened the door and went outside. She walked carefully to the third figure and knelt beside him. Solidus joined her and removed the figure's mask. He was a young man, about twenty, with dark hair and tan skin.

"Telatian." Rielle said. Solidus nodded.

"Why are you here?" He asked the young man. The young man looked fearfully at Solidus.

"We were sent to follow the Ambassador and discover her purpose. Then do anything necessary to keep her from success if it was meant to hinder our movements." Rielle's eyes grew wide. Solidus thought for a moment.

"Do you know who I am?" He asked. The young man shook his head. Solidus nodded. "I thought as much. I am a mage, my name would mean nothing to you so I won't even bother trying. I can use magic in many forms and, as you have just witnessed, I am also quite skilled with a blade." The young man nodded silently. Solidus scratched at his chin.

"I don't suppose you would go home if I asked you to, would you?" The young man shook his head.

"I cannot. I must fulfill my mission and return with honor, or not return at all." Solidus nodded.

"So you will try again if I let you go." The young man nodded but said nothing. Solidus sighed.

"I am sorry then." With a quick movement, Solidus thrust his sword through the young man's heart. The young man jerked once and then was still. Solidus removed his sword and wiped it clean on a red cloth before returning it to its scabbard. He looked at the sky then closed his eyes and breathed deeply through his nose, testing the air.

"Things are beginning to change." He said quietly after a few moments. "The decision has been made." Rielle felt dread in the pit of her stomach at Solidus's words.

"What decision?" She asked, almost inaudibly. Solidus sighed and turned back to Rielle.

"The decision that will force me to fight. Someone has given their soul to make a bid for power. That power will grow to overwhelm them and then destroy everything in its path unless it is stopped." Rielle shook her head to try and make sense of what Solidus was telling her.

"You are going to come and help us now? After telling me you wouldn't? What is this power that is so terrible that it has changed your mind so easily?" Solidus shook his head.

"Let us hope this crisis is turned aside before you have to find out." Solidus turned and walked toward the cabin. "Gather your things, young Rielle. We leave before nightfall."

4

Chapter Three

Rielle followed Solidus down the mountain path, to one side and a few steps behind the Hermit mage. The mountains were quiet, and even the constant wind did little to break the silence. Rielle grew restless and tried to strike up a conversation with her quiet companion.

"The Mercury Mountains are not as bad as the stories all say. It seems rather peaceful to me." Solidus chuckled without enthusiasm.

"I have set spells to protect the path from the base of the cliff to the cabin at the peak. When I came here I grew tired of fighting back the mountains very quickly. The stories you have heard about the mountains are probably much less frightening than the real thing." Rielle tried to imagine worse things than what she had heard.

"So there really are werewolves and ghosts and things?" Solidus nodded.

"Yes, but there are much more terrible things out there

than ghosts and werewolves. Things that, like me, the world has forgotten exist." Rielle faltered a step.

"Like what?" She asked tentatively. Solidus chuckled again, this time some emotion breaking through to the surface.

"You are very inquisitive. For now you don't need to know what is here. But to give you a taste, I will say that there are creatures here. Vile, evil creatures with insatiable bloodlust. And some of them are even older than I am." This almost stopped Rielle cold and she had to run a few steps to catch up to Solidus.

"Older than you?" Solidus nodded.

"By several hundred years." Rielle shivered.

"If they are so evil and bloodthirsty, why have they not left the mountains and killed everyone?" Solidus sighed to himself.

"I guess I should tell you. It is my duty as your master to teach you, and that is not limited only to magic. Do you know how the world was created?" Rielle thought back and managed to dredge up some memories from when she was young.

"My mother taught me that it was created by a supreme Deity." Solidus laughed.

"Are they still squabbling over Deities down below? The world was actually formed by Six Deities." Rielle shrugged.

"I was never one for religion." Solidus nodded.

"Which, until now, was a good decision. Even since I was amongst the rest of the world there has always been fighting about who's religion was correct. It was a rather nasty confrontation and is partly why I became a hermit. When I was much younger there were seven main religions, each contending for the spot of supreme truth." Rielle nodded.

"There are six that I know of now." Solidus nodded in return.

"I personally stamped out the seventh religion. Or at least I thought I had." Rielle stared at Solidus.

"You what?" Solidus rubbed his forehead.

"This is going to take a great deal more explanation than I had hoped for." He cleared his throat and glanced back at Rielle.

"In the beginning, Six Deities used their immense power to form the world out of chaos. Four of the Deities were rulers of the four elements, Wind, Water, Earth, and Fire. The last two Deities were Good and Evil. Though they are opposites they needed each other for balance and called the four elements together to help them create the world in a balanced manner. Using their combined powers, the Six called forth a great maelstrom that enveloped the chaos and separated it's elements. Then the six forced the elements to collide with one another, fusing them into a single mass." Solidus glanced back again and Rielle nodded to show she was keeping up with his story.

"The mass shifted and broke and healed itself several times until the elements became evenly balanced. This is how the Mercury Mountains were formed." Rielle suddenly looked a little lost. Solidus scratched his chin in thought.

"Think of it this way. Say you took a blanket and spread it out on the ground and found it was too big to fit where you wanted it to. So, you grabbed the blanket in the center and pulled it towards you. The blanket stays smooth where you pulled it, but the extra crumples and piles up in ridges and hills." Rielle envisioned the blanket and then nodded her understanding. Solidus continued.

"When the world finished forming the elements, though balanced, could not fit in the place allotted to them. So they collided and were thrust upward, creating the jagged formations of the Mercury Mountains." Rielle nodded.

"So it is like stepping in the sand? You step and the sand piles up on either side of your foot as it is displaced." Solidus nodded.

"Something like that. When the world had finished forming, each of the Six took a piece of it to shape in the way they saw fit. Each of these places reflected the element of the Deity that formed it. Plains for the Wind. Forests for Earth. Oceans for the Water. Deserts for Fire." Rielle thought for a moment and then an idea struck her.

"That sounds like the four great Kingdoms." Solidus nodded again.

"When human kind was created, groups of people flocked to each of the Deities and worshiped them as the creator of the world. That is what eventually caused the fight over which religion was correct. They all were right, but none of the humans would stop and think about it long enough to realize it. Eventually the people who worshipped the Deity of good became overzealous and could only see the rest of the world as evil. They planned to take over the world by force, and because they worshipped the Deity of good they had been blessed with incredible magical potential and would have been able to succeed. The world would have fallen to them and balance would have been thrown in to chaos. So, to keep the balance, the Deity of good caused their entire kingdom of Alenon to collapse into the sea. Save for a few individuals who, knowing that all the Deities had worked together in balance, prayed to their Deity for protection. Their Deity heard them and protected their small temple from the ocean's angry waters." Rielle was enthralled by the story and had to actively force herself to continue taking each step along the mountain path.

"Wouldn't sinking the Kingdom into the sea cause balance to shift anyway?" Solidus nodded.

"You are very perceptive. Yes, destroying the civilization would have thrown everything out of balance. However, The Deity of evil knew that all Six of the Deities relied on the balance to obtain their highest power. At the moment the Deity of good drowned the Kingdom of Alenon, the Deity of evil drew all of the evil creatures that worshipped it, and had been created by it, into the Mercury Mountains and Sealed them there." Rielle suddenly felt like she didn't like the Silence in the Mountains anymore.

"So that is why the creatures never come down from the mountains. But why are there still deaths near the mountain if they never come out?" Solidus looked out over the mountain range.

"The deaths are caused by normal creatures. Creatures that, out of desperation or hunger or any other number of reasons, strayed too close to the mountains and were corrupted by it, causing their bloodlust. I try to keep the incidents to a minimum and ward off the creatures, But I am only one person. I cannot be everywhere at once and sometimes a creature gets through and, regrettably, someone dies." Rielle was saddened but nodded anyway.

"I understand. At least you try." Solidus simply nodded. Rielle bit her lip nervously and hurriedly changed the subject.

"So there were Six Deities who created the world to achieve balance. And the people of the world gathered to them and created six main religions. But you said there was a seventh." Solidus nodded again.

"Yes, a seventh religion that did believe that the six Deities had created the world together." Rielle frowned.

"That doesn't seem too bad." Solidus scoffed.

"They believed that the world had been created by the Six, but they believed it should be returned to the state of chaos it had been in before it had been created." Rielle swallowed hard.

"So maybe it is bad then." Solidus harrumphed.

"They were fool hardy and even those who had worshipped the Deity of evil had feared them as dark beings. Each member of the religion, when they came of age, had a demon lodged inside of them."

"A demon?" Rielle shuddered at the thought. "I thought they were a myth." Solidus shook his head.

"No, demons are warped souls created from what is left of the chaotic energy left after the Maelstrom that created the world. When someone dies in this world their soul leaves their body and travels to a higher plane of existence. The place where the Six Deities exist. To get there they must travel through the chaos that existed before the world came to be. Sometimes a soul is taken by the chaotic energy and becomes corrupted and twisted, eventually becoming a demon if it cannot find its way back out. A way has been made now, a path that souls may follow, but some still fall from the path, and those who lost their way before are still within the chaos.

However, Demons cannot exist in either this world or the higher plane as they are consumed by chaos and each realm is built from balance. They must either be summoned and bound here, or given an opportunity to inhabit a living human body. The human gains great power, both physical and magical, in exchange for hosting the demon. However, if the human is particularly weak, or the demon particularly strong, the demon can corrupt and take over the human's body." Rielle shuddered again.

"Why would anyone want to risk such a fate?" She asked, almost sickened by the idea.

"Power." Solidus replied simply. "Imagine you could gain power like mine with no effort on your part. Simply host another being inside of you and suddenly you could level an army with the flick of your finger." Rielle looked at Solidus.

"You can level an army with a flick of your finger?" She asked in amazement. Solidus laughed.

"No, I was just trying to give you a reason why someone would sell themselves to a demon. They imagine they can gain such power. They don't understand how much practice it takes to gain such power, and how much more it takes to control it. Using power before they can control it could destroy them entirely. However that rarely happens because the demon won't let it's host use too much power at once. They may be twisted and, in most cases, evil. But they will protect their hosts to the best of their ability. They still need their host to anchor them to this world." Rielle nodded.

"I understand. So why did you destroy them?" Solidus cleared his throat.

"They were building an army. Summoning the most powerful demons they could control and placing them inside their followers. They planned to take the world and throw it severely out of balance so that the elements that formed the world would collapse and return to chaos." Rielle gasped.

"Why would they do such a thing? Wouldn't that destroy them as well?" Solidus shrugged.

"I can't claim to understand their intentions. Most of them believed that if the world were destroyed and thrown into chaos, then they would live solely in the higher plane. And a few that I fought did it only because they wished to cease existing." Rielle put one hand over her mouth.

"They are insane." Solidus nodded.

"Most assuredly. And until now I had thought all of them were destroyed." Rielle carefully thought through everything she had been told.

"If they are not all dead then..."

"They are still working from the shadows, still aiming for their goal." Solidus said. "This is all I will say for now. We will rest here for the night and set off again in the morning." Rielle glanced around and found that, during the course of their discussion, they had traveled all the way down the mountain and reached the clearing they had been in early that morning.

The sun was setting and the trees cast ominous shadows across the clearing. Rielle's eyes were drawn to the dead Felle Wolf. She resisted the urge to shudder again and nodded to Solidus.

"Ok, but can we camp a little further away from that?"

She asked, pointing at the wolf. Solidus half smiled, which angered Rielle and caused her cheeks to burn.

"As you wish. There is a place not far from here by the cliffs that will provide us with some shelter from the wind." Rielle nodded again and motioned for Solidus to lead the way.

* * *

The morning came quickly and Rielle didn't feel rested at all. She sat up, trying to work the kinks out of her neck and back, and saw Solidus bent over a small camp fire. He took things out of his pack a sprinkled them into a pan that was sizzling over the fire.

"There is a stream a little ways from here that pours out of the cliffs if you would like to wash." Solidus stated as he worked. Rielle marveled at how he had known she had woken up without turning to look.

She followed the cliff until she came to a small spring bubbling out of the cliffs. She knelt down beside the small pool created by the spring and quickly washed her hands and face.

"It will feel wonderful to get back to civilization where I can take a warm bath and sleep in a soft bed." She said to her reflection in the water. She sighed and thought back on the day before as she washed. Everything felt like a blur to her now.

It was difficult to grasp how much had happened to her in just a single day. She was a mage, the mountains she was sitting near were the domain of an evil deity, and a dead religion was trying to destroy the world by throwing it into chaos. She had met an old hermit who looked young and who was a powerful mage and skilled fighter.

"And a competent cook." Rielle reminded herself as the

smells of whatever Solidus had been cooking floated by her. She quickly finished then stood and returned to camp to find Solidus scooping a spoonful of something onto a plate. He held the plate out to Rielle and she took it. It tasted like nothing she had ever eaten, and looked like nothing she had ever seen, but it tasted good and she ate it without complaint.

Solidus was quiet for the rest of the morning. He quickly cleaned up the camp and set off into the trees, not waiting for Rielle to follow. Rielle rushed to follow the hermit and nearly had to jog to keep up with his pace.

Just before noon they came to a small village. The villagers greeted Solidus warmly and invited him to stay for lunch. He graciously accepted and introduced Rielle. The lunch was rushed but filling. Afterwards Solidus managed to barter for two horses to carry them the rest of the way to the small town that the allied armies were using as a base to protect the Southwestern Gate. They set out at a hard pace across the plains and Solidus started to ask Rielle questions.

"How large is the force the allied kingdoms have gathered?" Rielle counted the battalions in her head.

"Twenty thousand troops at either gate, give or take. There could be more now, I have been gone for more than a week." Solidus nodded.

"And how many troops do the Telatians control?" Rielle thought back to her briefing.

"At first there were a few thousand. After they were driven back they returned with reinforcements. They easily equaled the allied armies. It is all we can do now to keep them on the other side of the gate." Solidus nodded again and lowered his head in thought. Rielle, as curious as she was, chose to keep her questions to herself and let Solidus think. After a few miles Solidus grunted.

"Rielle." Rielle jerked awake and realized she had been nodding off.

"Yes?" She asked, shaking her head to clear it of sleep.

"Practice raising and lowering your shield. Let us see how proficient you can become by the time we reach our destination." Rielle nodded immediately and Solidus went back to his thoughts. Rielle focused on her inner power and began to make it build. It was difficult to do through the bouncing and jarring created by her horse's fast pace. Eventually she managed to build enough energy to create a shield around her. She felt the familiar pressure and, after a few minutes, released the shield again. She felt weakness enter her body and it was difficult to stay in her saddle. But, a few minutes later the weakness passed.

"Again." Solidus said without turning in his saddle. Rielle harrumphed and tried again. This time it wasn't as difficult to build her energy and it didn't take her quite as long to raise the shield. After she released the shield she felt the weakness again. And again, after she had recovered, Solidus called for her to repeat the process.

By nightfall, when they stopped to make camp, Rielle had discovered that Solidus, though kind and soft-spoken, was a difficult task master. He forced her to erect her shield over and over until she could build it without excessive amounts of thought. The whole day had been filled with Rielle raising and lowering it and raising it again when she had the strength. She felt exhausted.

Solidus built a small fire and prepared a meal. After eating, he cleaned up and then stood and began walking away from camp. Rielle jumped up to follow, but Solidus turned and held up a hand.

"You need your sleep." He told her simply. She frowned but nodded and laid down on her bed roll. Solidus nodded. "Sleep well, we will arrive at the Gate sometime tomorrow." Rielle sat upright.

"But how could we get so far so quickly?" Solidus pointed at the bedroll.

"Sleep." He told her again. Rielle scowled, laid back down, and watched as Solidus walked out into the darkness. Rielle rolled over, questions swimming in her head. But, eventually, her exhaustion overcame her curiosity and she drifted into sleep.

Chapter Four

Rielle woke to the sounds of Solidus cleaning up the camp. She sat up and stretched before yawning and looking around. The morning was crisp and clear and a cool breeze caused the long yellow grass to ripple in large waves across the plains. In the distance, Rielle could see the jagged cliffs of the Serpent Tongue Mountains rising into the air.

Though much smaller than the Mercury Mountains, the Serpent Tongue Mountains were a high, craggy, barren waste filled with wide chasms that were endlessly deep. Though many had tried, none had ever been able to pass over the mountains and into Telatia.

"We are already near the Serpent's Tongue?" Rielle asked. Solidus nodded and finished putting out the fire.

"The horses made good time yesterday. If we can keep that pace today, we should reach the main camp of the Allied Kingdoms before sundown." Solidus stood and tossed Rielle a small drawstring bag. When she looked at him questioningly he turned and mounted his horse.

"Breakfast." He said. "Eat while you ride. When you are done, practice raising and lowering your shield again." Rielle scowled and stood. She quickly tied her bedroll to her saddle and then mounted and followed behind Solidus. The bag Rielle had been given had a decent portion of dried meats and fruits. She sighed sadly, hoping Solidus had heard her, and began eating. When she had finished, Rielle quietly tucked the bag into a saddle bag and sat silently, hoping that Solidus had forgotten about her.

Solidus cleared his throat loudly. Rielle scowled at the back of his head then sighed and began building the energy for her shield. With each attempt, Rielle found that it was beginning to get easier to raise her shield. It took her less and less time each try, and she found that it did not tire her as much as it had the day before. At one point she could have sworn she saw Solidus watching her with a half smile on his face, but she only glimpsed him out of the corner of her eye and when she looked at him he was staring straight ahead.

By the time the sun had begun to sink low into the sky ahead of them, Rielle could raise and lower her shield in a matter of seconds, and the drain on her body no longer made her so tired she could not sit up straight. Rielle started to feel proud of her accomplishment and was going to tell Solidus so when she heard a war horn sound over the plains.

"We have arrived." Solidus stated, reigning his horse in. They walked their horses into town and left them at a stable near the gates. Solidus drew up the hood of his cloak and slung his bow over one shoulder.

"Take me to see the commander." He told Rielle. Rielle nodded and proudly led the way down the street towards the center of town. Most everyone who saw Rielle greeted her and stepped aside for her, and the soldiers stood aside and saluted as she passed. They came to a makeshift barricade at the edge of the town square. Beyond it, Rielle could see a large tent standing in the center and many smaller tents around it. Behind her she noticed that Solidus had suddenly stooped and began walking as if he were an old man. Taking little notice, she walked straight up to the guards at the barricade and showed them her signet ring.

"I bring a visitor to see the Commander and generals. I was informed that I was to see them immediately upon my arrival." The guards looked skeptical.

"The Commander and the Generals are in a meeting planning the assault on the Great Gate. We cannot let you pass." Rielle drew herself up and stared down the guard.

"I was sent on this diplomatic mission by the Commander and the three Kings of Laytrow, Hortaal, and Gentry." She waved her hand, making sure the signet ring that identified her as an ambassador flashed in the torchlight. "Perhaps you would like to explain to them why I was not admitted with this important noble visitor, and possible ally to the cause. I am sure they will be most understanding when devising a proper way to dispense punishment." Both guards jumped aside and saluted. Rielle nodded.

"Thank you gentlemen." She stuck her nose in the air importantly and walked past them. Solidus let out an inhuman growl as he passed the guards and chuckled to himself as they both jumped. Rielle strode up to the large tent and nodded to the guard. The guard saluted and then stepped inside the tent.

"Commander, Ambassador Rielle Lyvinius has arrived

and seeks audience." The guard announced. A mumbled reply was given and the guard stepped out and held the tent flap aside for Rielle and Solidus to pass. Rielle marched in without hesitation and Solidus followed, being careful to stay behind Rielle and as out of sight as possible.

Inside the tent was a large model of Galbrea, with more models representing cities, mountains, and armies. Four men in shining armor stood around the table talking. One general, a man of medium height with a short beard and green eyes, used a short stick to move the armies from the Hortaal side of the mountains to the Telatian side.

"We must strike quickly." He was saying. "If we can take the Telatian side of the Southwestern Gate we can set up a camp and be in a much better position to fight." Another general harrumphed. This second general was slightly taller than the first and was well muscled. He had a short beard of thick red hair and clear blue eyes.

"If we did that, then the Telatians would come at us from all sides and overwhelm us. Our only advantage at present is the fact that the Telatians can only come through the Gate pass a few dozen at a time." The first general scowled.

"You can't win a war by always playing on the defensive. When we reached the other side of the Gate we could use the full advantage of the Laytrow cavalry and mow down the Telatian forces with ease." The third general, a thin, balding man with grey hair and brown eyes, laughed.

"You put far too much faith in your cavalry, General Proteus." The general called Proteus scowled angrily and his face turned red. The fourth man in the tent, a large man with no beard and simple brown hair, finally spoke.

"Set the matter aside for now. Our ambassador has returned and what she has to say may change our plans entirely." The man turned and bowed to Rielle.

"Ambassador Rielle. I hope your journey was pleasant." Rielle laughed humorlessly.

"Hardly, Commander. The Telatians knew I was leaving. They sent a Felle wolf, and a team of Assassins to stop me."

"And yet you stand before us." Stated General Proteus. Rielle nodded shortly. "Indeed. The Felle wolf was shot down by a woodsman, though my guide was killed before he arrived. And the assassins met their end in the Mercury Mountains." The commander nodded.

"So the stories of the Mercury Mountains are true." Rielle nodded.

"The stories do not even begin to describe the horrors in those mountains." Solidus smiled to himself under his hood, amused with how Rielle toyed with her words and twisted his story to fit her purposes.

"And what of your mission?" Asked the second general. "Were you able to find evidence of the Hermit Mage?" Rielle scoffed.

"You could say I found evidence, yes." The general's eyes widened.

"So he does exist." Solidus laughed.

"Of course he exists." Rielle stepped aside and let Solidus shuffle in front of her. "He is me." The Commander placed one fist over his heart and bowed.

"We are honored that you have seen fit to grace us with your presence." Solidus nodded in return. The third general repeated his Commander's salute, but the other two generals stood unmoving.

"Have you no respect?" The third general asked the other two when he straightened. General Proteus scoffed.

"I will not bow to an unproven mystery man. Especially one who hides his features beneath a hood." The second General nodded his agreement.

"Though I do not want to appear disrespectful, I also do not want to foolishly give my allegiance to just any man, especially one who claims to be a mage." Rielle scowled.

"Are you saying that I have gone out and just found some strange man who can do magic tricks and brought him back, claiming he is the Hermit Mage?" The second general shook his head.

"I do not mean to say any such thing, Ambassador. Though most people agree that magic is an evil thing, I only say that I show my respect, but my allegiance is harder to earn."

"As befits a sailor of Gentry. Honest allies can be difficult to find and maintain, especially on the open sea." Solidus stated. The second general nodded to Solidus. "Indeed, though how you knew I was a Gentry is a mystery to me." Solidus tapped the side of his head.

"I have been around a long time. I can see your heritage in your features, even if others mistake them for the same as the Laytrow Plainsman standing beside you." General Proteus scoffed.

"Discovering our nationality is no hard task. It is going to take a lot more to impress me."

"Oh?" Solidus asked mockingly. "And just what would impress you, General Proteus?" The general scowled at Solidus.

"For starters you could show your face, or are you too much of a coward to show yourself among Men? Or maybe you are just disfigured and ugly and cannot bare to show your face in public."

"That is enough, General Proteus." The Commander ordered. General Proteus fell unwillingly silent. Solidus waved one hand.

"It is of little consequence, Commander. A face is something many people must see to trust. Even your young ambassador here would not trust me as her guide through the mountains until I had shown her my face." Solidus straightened his posture and squared his shoulders before reaching up and removing his hood. The Commander and the third general's eyes widened and the remaining two generals were openly shocked.

"He is a boy!" General Proteus exclaimed.

"Indeed, it does seem difficult to see this young man as an ageless mage." The second general agreed.

"I am also surprised by your youthful appearance." The Commander stated. "But I also know that Rielle is an intelligent young woman and an excellent ambassador. She would not have brought you here if she did not wholeheartedly believe you are who you claim to be."

"I agree." Stated the third general.

"Well I do not." General Proteus raged. "I will not listen to a young whelp who claims he is older and wiser than any of us in this tent." Solidus shrugged.

"That is your choice to make, but you would be very unwise to brush me aside so quickly. You will have need of me very soon." General Proteus harrumphed.

"I have no need for an unproven boy." Solidus half smiled.

"Then you wish to fight the warrior who has just broken through your ranks on your own? You may find him too skilled for you." General Proteus took in a breath to angrily criticize Solidus when a soldier burst into the tent.

"Commander! A Telatian soldier has just broken our front line. Reinforcements have been sent, but no one can stop him. If he isn't stopped quickly he could weaken the front enough to allow the Telatians to break through!" Solidus nodded.

"Thank you Soldier, your Commander very much appreciates this information. Return to your battalion and be ready in case an attack does come from the Telatians." The Soldier saluted and rushed from the tent. Solidus turned back to General Proteus.

"I suggest you hurry before any more of your soldiers are killed. Don't forget your weapon and your helmet on the way out." General Proteus scowled and rushed from the tent. Solidus turned to the other generals.

"It may be wise to come and witness this confrontation. It will show you what you are truly fighting against." Solidus turned and looked directly at Rielle. "Lead the way, Rielle. You will not wish to miss this." Rielle nodded, a little numb from Solidus's commanding air. She left the tent, followed by Solidus, the Commander, and the remaining two generals, and quickly headed towards the Great Gate.

Even from a distance, the great structure that stretched across the two sides of the narrow pass between the mountains was easily visible in the evening light. The Great Southwestern Gate consisted of two massive stone pillars that rose hundreds of feet into the air with an arch between them.

Though not actually a gate, it had barred the way in and out of Telatia for a hundred generations.

General Proteus's path was easy to follow. Solidus almost chuckled to himself as they passed fallen and angry looking soldiers beside the path being lifted up by their comrades. Soon they all heard the sounds of fighting. Grunts and shouts and sounds of steel striking steel filled the air and then a voice raised over the commotion.

"Does no one in this army know how to fight? You are all weak." More shouting was heard and a roar filled the air.

"Here! Fight me and we shall see who is weak." Rielle arrived just in time to see General Proteus step out into the open to confront the Telatian soldier. The Telatian was a tall, thin man wielding two long, curved blades. He wore black chain mail armor from head to toe and had a black cloth wrapped around his head and face, leaving only his eyes uncovered.

"A general? Perhaps this will entertain me." Rielle noticed a slight hiss to the man's voice. She jumped slightly as Solidus placed a hand on her shoulder.

"Watch him carefully." He whispered only for her to hear. Rielle nodded carefully and turned her eyes back on General Proteus and the Telatian. General Proteus drew a large two handed sword from a scabbard at his waist and held it easily before him.

"I will do more than entertain you." He said smugly. Rielle could tell, just by looking at his eyes, that the Telatian was smiling. The soldiers all stepped back to make room for the duel, and room was made for the Commander and the Generals to stand close to the center of the circle.

After a few moments of fighting the Commander turned his back on the duel. The Telatian danced nimbly around the angry General and made quick jabbing thrusts with his swords. General Proteus could not hit the Telatian no matter how hard he tried, which angered him further and caused him to become more and more reckless in his attacks. After only minutes of fighting, General Proteus began to lag as the many small cuts he was accumulating were causing him to lose great amounts of blood. Finally Rielle could bear watching no longer.

"Help him." She said quietly. "Help him, please." She turned and looked at Solidus who sadly watched the fight drag on.

"It is not my place to intervene. He does not want me to fight this fight."

"He may not." The Commander said. "But I do. I ask that you help us fight this fight. I cannot lose one of my generals like this. General Proteus's pride is not worth his life."

"Please." Rielle repeated. Solidus took a long, deep breath and then handed his bow to Rielle, along with his cloak.

"Watch, Rielle, so that you may learn." He said before walking casually into the open area where the fight was taking place. General Proteus dropped to his knees and desperately tried to swing his heavy sword. The Telatian easily knocked it aside and it skittered along the ground and into the crowd of soldiers. The Telatian stood over the general triumphantly.

"If you are the best this army has to offer, then it is a wonder we haven't destroyed you already."

"I would normally agree with you." Solidus said conversationally. "But seeing as you are not a typical human, I can imagine that you must be irate with your own army as well." The Telatian looked up and watched Solidus walk out into the center of the circle.

"It must be so hard not to become frustrated and disobey orders from your superiors, knowing that you could do so much better than they." The Telatian said nothing. Solidus grinned knowingly. "To take out those frustrations on a worthy opponent, would that not be most agreeable?" The Telatian turned towards Solidus.

"What did you have in mind?" Solidus motioned with one hand.

"You let the general go and suffer with his wounds, and you can fight me. I may provide you with more entertainment than he." The Telatian stood in silence for a moment and then nodded.

"This arrangement is satisfactory." Solidus looked at a few soldiers and nodded. They immediately ran out and carried the general back off of the field. The Telatian turned and faced Solidus in a fighting stance.

"Draw your weapon." He said. Solidus nodded.

"I will do so when it becomes necessary. You may proceed." The Telatian shrugged and charged at Solidus with incredible speed. Rielle was sure he was going to be killed, but at the last possible moment, Solidus drew his curved sword and blocked both enemy swords in mid stroke. The Telatian laughed hysterically.

"Excellent, Perhaps you will provide me with some entertainment after all." He jumped back and swung at Solidus once again. Solidus expertly parried the attack and sidestepped another. The Telatian danced back and forth, circling Solidus, who stood still and waiting.

The Telatian attacked as he had General Proteus, with quick jabbing strikes, but Solidus easily deflected or avoided each blow. After a short time, it was obvious that the Telatian had began to get frustrated and each one of his attacks became more and more thought out. After a few minutes of fighting, Solidus watched as the Telatian carefully stalked around him.

"Do you grow impatient? Frustrated? Would you prefer that I end this fight, or continue fighting as we are?" The Telatian continued to circle.

"You have made your point. You are a skilled warrior. Don't waste both of our time stalling this fight. Fight or surrender." Solidus bowed, his eyes never leaving the Telatian.

"As you wish." Solidus rushed the Telatian and, with two swift, fluid movements, he disarmed him. Another strike sent him to the ground, and a final blow ended the fight. Everyone stood watching in awe. Solidus motioned to Rielle and she walked out and stood beside him. Solidus sheathed his sword and then untied the scabbard from his waist and held it out to Rielle.

"Hold this." Rielle nodded and took the sword and then took a step back as Solidus knelt down beside the dead man. Solidus pressed both hands together as if he were praying and bowed his head and began to chant something that Rielle did not understand. Seconds passed and Solidus began to glow. The crowd of soldiers watching gasped and backed further away as the glow grew brighter.

Solidus raised his head and pulled his hands apart slowly,

causing the air to ripple between them as if it were water. Suddenly the air grew cold and Rielle's breath came in puffs of steam. Then the air above the dead Telatian rippled and twisted, forming a shape. The shape continued to twist until it became a horrific image.

A creature with deep orange skin, a yellow tongue, and slick black spikes protruding from its body solidified above Solidus as he chanted. After a few moments, Solidus stopped chanting and stood, his hands still held apart.

"What is your name?" He asked. The creature hissed at him. Solidus pressed his hands closer together and the creature suddenly shrieked in pain. "What is your name?" Solidus repeated. The creature glared at him.

"Bortrinaumilus." It hissed. Solidus nodded.

"How long has this body played your host?" The creature hissed again.

"Half a moon." A strange expression fluttered across Solidus's face, but quickly disappeared.

"Answer me one more question and I may send you back to the Chaos rather than simply destroying you. Who is responsible for your summoning?" The creature struggled with itself for a few moments before shaking itself in frustration.

"A Priest in a black temple at the center of a high city of tiers." Solidus nodded.

"Very well then." He began to chant again and, after a few phrases, he forced his hands together again, causing a shockwave of energy to pulse from his body. The creature shattered and disappeared into the air. The soldiers stood and watched in awe as Solidus took his sword back from Rielle and tied it at his waist.

"Your time could be better spent standing at your posts before the gate." Solidus called out to the crowd as he fastened his cloak back on. Immediately several captains could be heard shouting orders for their soldiers to return to their positions. The crowd of soldiers dispersed quickly and Solidus slipped his bow back over his shoulder. He turned back and fixed a piercing gaze on the Commander and his two generals standing over the injured General Proteus.

"Do I meet with your approval?" He asked. All three men bowed deeply and General Proteus looked away in shame. Solidus nodded once shortly and walked past them, Rielle following closely behind.

"We may continue our discussion in your war pavilion." He said over his shoulder to them. Rielle followed a step behind Solidus, marveling at the amount of authority he controlled, even among men such as the generals and the Commander.

6

Chapter Five

Solidus sat at the table containing the model of the country and listened as the generals explained what had been done up until that point in the war. His sharp eyes followed as they pointed out each position of each battle and the outcome. When they had finished, Solidus sat quietly thinking over everything.

A meal was brought and was eaten in silence. Once it was finished and had been cleared away, Solidus went back to thinking. Rielle shifted back and forth nervously, dreading what would come out of Solidus's mouth the next time he spoke. Finally Solidus stood.

"How prepared are you for a full scale invasion?" Solidus asked. The Commander sat up straighter.

"What do you mean?" Solidus looked down at the model.

"The warrior who broke your lines today, was a demon host. You watched as I drew the creature from him, and then sent it back into the void after he had died. They are beginning to seal demons inside hosts to create stronger soldiers.

In a single, short month they will over run you and invade. My question is, are your cities ready for invasion? Are they ready to be defended and resist siege?" The grey haired general stood slowly from his seat.

"Are you sure they will attack so soon?" Solidus nodded.

"What do you know of the Blood Moon Cycle?" General Proteus snorted from his chair. He had insisted that he be placed in the tent so he could be part of the planning.

"It is a myth." Solidus nodded.

"And so am I, General." General Proteus turned his head away and said nothing. Rielle thought back on all the books she had ever read, searching for an answer to Solidus's question.

"There are multiple moon cycles." She recalled. "Storm cycle, Ice cycle, Harvest cycle, and many others. Most only happen once a year or every other year. But I have never heard of the Blood cycle." Solidus nodded.

"It was never commonly taught, even before I went into exile. The Blood Moon Cycle happens only once every few hundred years, and it is very dangerous."

"How so?" The Commander asked. Solidus cleared his throat.

"Rielle will remember this, but the world depends on balance. The greatest strengths come from balance. During most time, life is a dominant force in the world. But to maintain balance, every few hundred years, a Blood Moon occurs. During that short period of time, Death becomes the dominant force in this world. Demons grow in strength, even a minor injury can be fatal, and blood can be absorbed to make others stronger. On the night of the Blood Moon Cycle, the Telatian army will become unimaginably strong. If you stand in their way, you will be killed and your blood will be absorbed to make them even stronger and more bloodthirsty. If you wish to survive that night it would be best if you were inside your cities and prepared for the worst." The grey haired general slipped back into his chair.

"It would take months of preparation and require that we leave the Southwestern Gate untended." Solidus turned and motioned for Rielle to follow.

"You have close to a month before the Blood Moon Cycle begins, I suggest you make the most of your time." The Commander quickly stood.

"What are you going to do?" Solidus glanced back over his shoulder as he left the tent.

"I am going to destroy the Great Southwestern Gate."

* * *

Rielle watched as soldiers quickly packed up their camps and moved away from the Great Gate. A short ways away, Solidus stood contemplating the structure that formed the Southwestern Gate.

"Can you do it?" Rielle asked him. Solidus nodded.

"It is not a question of if I can do it. It is a question of how."

"How?" Rielle questioned. Solidus nodded again.

"Bringing down the Gate is not an issue. I need to bring it down and make it impassable to the Telatians. It would do no good to destroy the Gate and have the Telatians simply climb over the rubble." Rielle nodded her understanding. They stood quietly, Rielle listening to the army as it moved away.

"Are you prepared to follow me?" Solidus asked suddenly. Rielle looked up at his sad face.

"Of course. Why wouldn't I be?" She asked him. Solidus stared straight ahead.

"We will be going into places that are very dangerous and unsavory. You will see things that could drive you to the edge of your sanity. You will be in grave danger and I won't guarantee that I will be able to protect you all of the time." Rielle swallowed and took a deep breath before nodding.

"I understand. I will still follow you." Solidus nodded.

"Then we head into the wastes of Telatia." Rielle nodded and shakily followed Solidus into the Southwestern Gate. The walk through the gate was tedious. Solidus walked along slowly, looking around at the narrow passage of the Gate.

"It has been a very long time since I walked through here. Almost eight hundred years now." He said conversationally. Rielle's jaw dropped in spite of herself.

"Eight hundred years?" Solidus nodded with a chuckle.

"Yes, I walked through here on the way to my exile in the Mercury Mountains." Rielle counted back, trying to remember her history lessons.

"Eight hundred years ago, that was just after the Purge. The crusade to destroy all Magic users." Solidus nodded.

"You know your history, good. Yes, I kept out of sight during the Purge, helping those I could to escape the slaughter. After it was over, I made a visit to many places all over Galbrea so that I could remember them while in exile. I traveled through Gentry, Telatia, Hortaal, and Laytrow before entering the Mercury Mountains and cleansing the evil from the highest peak." Solidus continued walking slowly through the dark passages in silence. Rielle walked behind Solidus, deep in thought. Eventually, curiosity overcame her and she coughed once before speaking.

"Solidus?"

"Hmm?" Solidus seemed lost in his own thoughts. Rielle toyed with her hands for a few moments before finally asking,

"How old are you?" Solidus chuckled.

"Ageless." He told her. Rielle made a disapproving sound.

"I know that. I meant how long has it been since you were born?" Solidus glanced back with one eyebrow raised.

"That isn't exactly the most pertinent information at the moment." Rielle shrugged.

"I was just curious. You told me you had taught High King Hortaal Lyvinius. If that is true, you would have to be at least fifteen hundred years old." Rielle took a few steps before she realized the gravity of what she had said.

"Fifteen hundred years!? Are you really that old?" She asked, her steps faltering for a moment. Solidus chuckled.

"If you must know, I am better than twice that." Rielle stopped in her tracks.

"Three thousand!?" Solidus nodded and kept walking. Rielle stood still for a moment and then shook herself and rushed to catch up to Solidus.

"You are really three thousand years old?" Solidus chuckled again.

"Three thousand eight hundred, give or take a dozen or so years. You tend to lose track when you get as old as I am." Rielle stared at Solidus as they walked. After a little ways, Solidus spoke again.

"Staring at me won't make me look any older." Rielle

blushed furiously and looked down at her feet, locking them there until she stepped onto blank sand. Looking up she found they had left the pass and had entered a vast desert. She looked around, expecting to see a thousand telatian soldiers, but found nothing but empty, windblown sand.

"Where is the Telatian army?" She quickly tried to inspect the mountains to either side, expecting to find hundreds of soldiers rushing down to ambush them. The desert was still.

"There isn't anyone around." Rielle stated, wondering if she might believe it if she voiced it again. Solidus simply nodded.

"There were not near as many Telatians as there seemed to be. When they returned to attack the gates a second time, their numbers had not actually increased. There were simply Demon hosts among them, which made the army stronger and appear to have more soldiers."

"Even so." Rielle said, once again looking around. "We can't have reduced their armies down to a single man." Solidus shook his head.

"They sent him to see if a stronger Demon host would be sufficient to break the lines and allow them to pass through the gate. It takes time and energy to seal a Demon to a human host. They sent him, and a few others, to see what would be needed to break the lines. That way they could prepare for a full scale assault with a much higher chance of success." Rielle nodded and thought over Solidus's explanation for a moment before speaking again.

"Ok, but shouldn't there still be some sort of force on this side of the gate? They surely wouldn't leave it undefended so that the allied kingdoms could gain a foothold here... would they?" Solidus smiled.

"It is good to know you can think things through, and yes, there was a small force here. When they witnessed my arrival, and watched what I did to the Demon after the fight, they retreated to bring the news to their leader. As for why they would leave the gate entirely undefended, there are several reasons. The soldiers from the other kingdoms are not accustomed to the conditions here in the desert. The sand would severely slow their march, the heat would tire the men and horses, and there are... other dangers here. The Telatians know this and don't consider the other kingdoms as much of a threat in such conditions. Now, does that answer all of your questions? We should move on." Rielle nodded slowly and followed behind Solidus when he moved.

They walked a few hundred feet away from the Gate and then Solidus turned around and held his arms out to either side of him, the palms of his hands turned up.

Rielle watched in wonder as silver strings of energy appeared in Solidus's hands, attached to the end of each finger. The strings extended deep into the pass they had just left.

“What are they?” Rielle asked, pointing at the silver strings.

“Energy I have attached at intervals through the entire length of the gate. They are what I will use to pull down the pass. Now please be silent, I must concentrate.” Solidus closed his eyes and began mumbling to himself. Rielle pursed her lips, and vowed to herself that she wouldn't ask any more questions. As Solidus continued, his mumbling became a rumble and his fingers began to twitch. Back and forth, they moved individually, causing the magical strings attached to them to quiver.

A rumble sounded from deep within the gate, and Rielle's eyes widened as the sound grew louder and louder until it had become an earth shaking roar. Solidus raised his hands above his head, as if he were a puppet master, controlling a puppet on the end of its strings. His voice rose and he spoke a few words that were foreign to Rielle before gathering all the strings into a single tight fist and pulling down and back.

A great groan issued from the mountain and then a gigantic crack, as if the world itself was splitting apart, as the mountains and the Gate collapsed. Dust and sand rose into the air, blinding Rielle and causing her to cough and quickly cover her face with her cloak. Rielle could barely make out Solidus in the sudden dust storm as he continued to flick his fingers, guiding something with the silver threads in his hands. After what seemed like an eternity to Rielle, the roaring and the groaning eased to a stop and Solidus placed his hands at his sides, the silver strings vanishing.

With a slow breath, Solidus made a downward motion and the dust quickly settled. Rielle stood in shock, staring at the scene before her. The Great Southwestern Gate was gone. It was almost as if it had never been there at all. In its place stood a massive rockslide of boulders the size of houses that piled up nearly as high as the mountain itself.

The slide was steep, like a cliff face, and the boulders were wedged so tightly together that Rielle didn't think they could ever be moved. Solidus took a few slow, deep breaths and then opened his eyes.

"The Telatians should find crossing the pass to be difficult now." Rielle nodded mutely. Solidus placed one hand on her shoulder and turned her to look at him.

"This is what can be done with study, practice, and balance. Remember that and you will grow strong in your skill." Rielle stared blankly at Solidus.

"I could never..." Solidus nodded.

"Probably not, but you will never need to. Magic on this scale is not something that should be done lightly. The balance of the elements can be broken if it is not done correctly. A wrong move could cause imbalance and would have to be compensated for elsewhere." Rielle slowly started to recover.

"Elsewhere?" Solidus nodded and steered her away from the gate, walking towards the open desert.

"If the elements had been thrown out of balance here, somewhere else the elements would have to change to keep the world in balance. If I had not been careful pulling down this mountain, another might have been thrust up out of the sea to compensate. Performing magic, any magic, on a large scale can have cataclysmic consequences. You must remember that and always bear the consequences in mind when using your power. Balance must remain." Rielle nodded as they walked away from the devastated Gate.

"Good. Now, you need your rest. This journey will be difficult on you." As Rielle started to mutter a reply, Solidus waved one hand across her face and her eyes fluttered shut. He led her along as she slept, keeping her upright and walking towards the Northeast as the sky darkened.

* * *

Rielle was more confused than she had ever been in her entire life. She stood before the gates of an enormous tiered city constructed of black stone. She had no memory of traveling to this city. She remembered speaking with Solidus at the Southwestern Gate after it had been destroyed. The next thing she knew, she was opening her eyes to see the massive desert city laid before her.

"Where are we? How did we get here?" She asked. Solidus answered from beside her. "We have arrived at Tyr 'anon. The capital city of Telatia." Rielle shook her head.

"We cannot have made it here so quickly." Solidus chuckled.

"You have been asleep for three days." Rielle turned to Solidus.

"Three days? How is that possible?" Solidus looked on with seemingly little concern.

"I placed you in an enchanted sleep that has lasted three days. You needed rest and we could not afford to delay. I simply led you along as you slept." Rielle was suddenly angry.

"But for three days? Couldn't you have let me wake up and carry myself under my own power?" Solidus shook his head.

"For now, all you need to know is that there are things in this desert that it is best to avoid. Ancient things that recognize me and would have harmed you, had you been conscious for the encounter." Most of Rielle's conviction drained away.

"I would still have preferred to have the choice." She tried to sound angry. Solidus shrugged.

"Traveling with me means you will have to endure a great many things you would not otherwise choose to experience. That is the choice you have made in following me." Rielle resisted the urge to stamp her foot.

"You started to teach me magic, and I accepted you as my

teacher. I am not going to leave until you have fully trained me. I accepted the fact that I can use magic and now I am going to learn to do so. I don't care if I enjoy it or not." Solidus half smiled.

"That will have to wait until we are done here. Most of the people here are very... zealous when it comes to magic. Nearly as much as the people of Hortaal. Should they even begin to suspect we are magic users it will become very difficult to get out of the city without casualties. The few who are not against magic users are magic users themselves or demon hosts. In either case, they already know we are here. And in both cases they are not happy we have come." Rielle turned back and looked at the city. The black stone made it look dark and foreboding.

"If they do not want us here, what is stopping them from trying to drive us out of the city?"

"Because those of us who know what you are also know who you are." Called a voice from the shadow of the city gate. A tall, thin man with tan skin and dark hair stepped out into the open. He was wrapped, head to toe, in sand colored cloth to protect him from the morning sun. The figure spoke again.

"No one in his right mind would challenge Grandmaster Solidus, The Silver Mage. Not in the open, and especially not anywhere near Tyr 'anon. Not even the High Priest would risk that." Solidus nodded slightly.

"I would see your master. We have something to discuss." The man looked at Solidus. "I'm afraid my master sends his apologies on that point. He cannot meet with you right now as something of great importance currently holds his attention." Solidus fixed the man with a solid gaze.

"Then tell your master he had better find a moment that his attention is not occupied. I will speak with him. If he refuses, He will not have to worry about risking a confrontation openly in the city, because I will." The man met his gaze for a few moments and then turned away.

"I will speak with my master." Solidus nodded.

"Good. I will be waiting for his reply in the inn on the third tier, below the temple. He has until sundown to find the time to meet with me, Or I will make time for him." The man nodded, then swept around and back through the way he had come. Solidus motioned and Rielle followed him through the gate and into the city.

As she followed Solidus through the city, Rielle noticed that it had been designed specifically for war. Each building was built at equal intervals around the city, and each successive building was higher than the one before it to allow for archers and soldiers to stand and fight. The streets below were narrow with no places to hide from sight.

Each tier of the city was thirty feet higher than the tier below and had a wall that spanned the entire length of the raised section. The only way up to each tier was a slender staircase that led up the side of the wall and would be easily defended from all directions.

By the time they had reached the inn Solidus had mentioned, Rielle was feeling very depressed from looking at the black stone and worn from the long walk across the city.

"How was a city like this ever conceived?" She asked, as she sat down at a table in the corner that Solidus motioned to.

"Tel'a Gromai Shia, the Empress who founded Telatia, did not trust the leaders of the other five kingdoms. Though the deities had commanded their followers that there should be peace, Tel'a could not bring herself to trust that the peace would last long. She created the city so that any number of soldiers could defend it from any of the three tiers, and then commanded that any other cities be built adjacent to the capital.

Her initial intent was to protect her people, but her advisor, Borsa Kera Moradon, killed the empress in her sleep and took control of the kingdom." Rielle stared at Solidus for several moments in silence as he ordered some food and drink from a maid.

"What did the counselor do after he took control?" She asked him, after the maid had left. Solidus cleared his throat and leaned back in his chair.

"To gain the support of the people, he claimed assassins had attacked the empress in her bedchamber and killed her. Then he 'humbly' took control of the kingdom and named it after the empress. Tel'a-Shia, or Telatia. He then converted the palace into a temple and became the first priest, and demon host, of the Chaos Order." Rielle shook her head.

"I never cared for Telatian politics. And their names are far too complicated for my taste." Solidus chuckled.

"Don't tell that to a Telatian. Their names hold great significance for them. Each part of their name has a different meaning and honor attached to it. But right now I haven't the time, or the desire, to try and teach you their complex naming system. As for their system of politics, the more complicated they are, the more likely they are to get what they want from others. Especially so if they can claim dishonor because of a broken rule or custom." Rielle sat back as the maid returned with two plates of steaming meat and vegetables, and two tankards of spiced cider. When the maid had once again departed, Rielle sat forward and spoke as Solidus began to eat.

"Then how is it you got the man at the gate to go and speak with the priest to gain you an audience. You didn't even come close to Telatian protocol." Solidus chuckled and then took a drink of his cider to wash down a mouthful of food.

"The Priest and I do not stand on protocol. The priest, because he rules the kingdom and city, I because I have power and knowledge. That gives me weight to throw around. The man at the gate simply does not wish to get in the way of either me, or the priest." Rielle stared at her plate with a puzzled look on her face.

"How is it that so many know who you are?" Solidus shrugged and wiped his mouth.

"As thorough as the Purge was, it did not utterly destroy all magic users or texts on magic. As I mentioned before, I helped many escape myself. Those attuned to magic can sense my aura and can, thus, identify me. They know of me either by word of mouth, by the teachings of their masters, or by reading texts which contain my name and description. That or they are demon hosts. All demons remember me well, there are no secrets in the chaos. And though most may know me, there are also magic users here who only know that I hold great power and they will not risk their lives trying to steal knowledge or attack. They know better." Rielle nodded. She suddenly found herself ravenously hungry and quickly began to eat.

They didn't have to wait long before the Telatian who had

met them at the gate returned. He whispered a few words to Solidus, who nodded, then he turned and left. Solidus let Rielle quickly finish eating and then motioned for her to follow.

They left the inn and made their way through the few people who wandered the top tier of the city. Moments later Rielle found herself standing at the bottom of a long stairway that led up to the temple entrance. Two guards stepped in to block their path.

"What business do you have at the temple?" One of the guards asked gruffly. Solidus kept his eyes downcast.

"We have been summoned to see your high priest." He told the guard. The guard scoffed. "I have been ordered by the high priest himself not to allow anyone to disturb him today." Solidus kept his eyes firmly on the ground.

"We have a matter of great importance to speak of with the high priest." The guard shook his head with a growl and placed one hand on the sword at his side.

"And I have told you, I am to let no man pass." Solidus stood silently for a moment and then raised his head and fixed his eyes on the guard.

"If I were you, I would not risk the ire of both myself and the high priest by barring our passage." The guard flinched back from Solidus's piercing gaze.

"If the high priest commands it, we will let you pass." The guard replied, and both guards quickly stepped aside. Solidus quickly led Rielle past the guards and up the long stairway. Rielle was still amazed by the air of command that Solidus seemed to hold over everyone they met, but she was careful not to let her amazement show on her face. Solidus all but marched up to the temple doors. The guards there hurriedly pushed open the doors and scrambled to get out of Solidus's way. Rielle almost grinned until Solidus spoke.

"Stay close." He grumbled. Rielle jumped and found herself trying to crowd closer to the mage. Inside the temple, the stone seemed even darker than it had been outside. Sputtering torches lined the walls but did little to light their way or warm the chilling air. The air itself felt dirty to Rielle, like oil on water, and she wanted nothing more than to scrub away the filth. But the deeper into the temple they went, the stronger the feeling became.

"It is the taint of the Chaos brought here by summoning demons and binding them to hosts." Solidus said as they walked. Rielle shuddered and then promised herself she would stop shuddering. They walked through winding hallways with other halls branching off in seemingly absurd directions. Eventually they came to a tall door with strange symbols etched into its surface. In front of that door stood the tall Telatian man who had met them when they entered the city.

Solidus stopped before the door and glanced at the man. The man nodded and quickly entered the room beyond. Several seconds went by and then he returned and motioned Solidus through the door. Rielle followed quickly behind and cringed as the doors banged shut behind them.

The room was large and richly decorated. Expensive furniture from every part of the world sat expertly positioned around the edge of the room. The center was empty, save for a wide circle, with symbols all around it, drawn on the floor. At the other end of the room was an altar and before it stood a man of medium height and strong build. He had black hair with streaks of gray beginning to show but he stood as if he were still in his prime.

"To be visited by such a powerful guest as you, Grandmaster Solidus, it defies the imagination." The voice was silky and quiet and Rielle felt strangely drawn to it.

"I didn't come here on a social call, Borsa, and you know that." The man sighed and turned around. Rielle was stunned. The high priest was possibly the most handsome man she had ever seen. His face was strong and well defined, his eyes a pale blue almost as clear as Solidus's silver eyes, and his smile seemed to cut into Rielle and make her want to smile too. Solidus remained passive, seemingly ignorant of the priest's looks.

The priest, to Rielle's satisfaction, seemed a little nervous and unable to maintain eye contact with Solidus for more than a few seconds at a time. To Rielle's dismay, however, he chose to look at her instead.

"Who is this one you have brought with you Master Solidus? She seems very young, and somehow familiar." Solidus nodded.

"Perhaps. She is a high ranking Ambassador of Hortaal." The priest nodded as if he had expected no less. "She also has the potential and is under my tutelage." The priest's eyes widened almost unnoticeably for a moment and then returned to normal.

"I see. So she is not here to negotiate for the Allied kingdoms then?" Solidus shook his head.

"No, she is not. She is simply accompanying me. But there

has been enough of this stalling already." The priest nodded, almost reluctantly.

"Indeed. Why have you come here Master Solidus? It is unheard of for you to leave the Mercury Mountains." Solidus nodded.

"Yes, and I would have been content with staying there and letting events unfold. But you changed that." The priest took on a curious look.

"Oh? And how, pray tell, did I do that?" Solidus's expression did not change.

"Five days ago you made a choice. A decision that could have very dangerous, and very far reaching effects" A dark expression flashed across the priests features. If she had not been trained to spot such things, Rielle thought she might have missed it.

"What manner of choice do you think I could have made that would have such repercussions?" The priest asked, a little too calmly. The corner of Solidus's mouth twitched, almost as if to smile.

"You think you have found a demon worthy of having you as a host." The priest's false smiled turned into an angry scowl.

"Who is to say I am not already a host?" Solidus laughed emotionlessly.

"You have made a connection, Borsa, but you don't yet have the strength to tear the demon from the Chaos and seal it within your body. That is why you wait for a Blood Moon Cycle. You can guess at its timing, but you cannot know. It could be hours or years before the Blood Moon comes." The Priest's scowl deepened.

"I will wait as I must. And who are you to tell me I am

wrong? Who are you to tell me that destroying this world will not bring me glory in the next?" Solidus also scowled and his gaze, much to Rielle's surprise, seemed to sharpen further.

"You do not understand what would happen if balance was lost. Your body itself is balance. A body made from Earth, willed to life by Fire, and sustained by Water and Air. Losing that would destroy you, not take you to the heaven realm. Your body would join the chaos and you would not be your own to command anymore. You still have a chance to undo what you have done. You are not yet completely under the demon's sway. If you break the connection now you can save yourself and avoid the senseless destruction you plan." For a moment, Rielle almost thought Solidus had gotten to the priest with his words. But after a few moments the scowl returned.

"You are not one to judge me. One who nearly severed the bond between the elements of the world. One who nearly broke the world and sent it spiraling back into chaos." Solidus saddened visibly and suddenly Rielle could see a great burden weighing him down, though what that burden was she could not say. Solidus looked back at the priest, the sharpness in his eyes returning.

"Had I not risked breaking the world apart, the Chaos order would have done so without remorse. Had your predecessor made the choice I have warned you to make, and severed his connection with his demon, then the demons would not have come to overrun this place and I would not have been forced to act." Even the priest now visibly flinched from the power in Solidus's voice and gaze, and Rielle could only stand

and watch, in awe of the struggle of power going on before her eyes. The priest only partially recovered.

"Your words will not turn me from my path. My way is set and I will not deviate." Solidus sighed and removed his gaze from the priest.

"So be it. I still give you the chance to turn away. Make the choice and sever your connection before you destroy yourself. If you do not make the choice before the Blood Moon Cycle, I will return, and the choice will be made for you." Solidus motioned to Rielle and they turned to leave the room.

Had Rielle chanced a look back, she might have seen the anger building in the priest's face. Had Solidus not had an incalculable weight on his mind he might have sensed the attack before it came. As it was, he could only turn as the priest hurled a dagger from beneath his robe. The dagger flashed through the air and met Rielle in the center of her back between her shoulder blades. She gasped and fell forward, dropping to the ground, unconscious before she struck the black stone floor.

With supreme effort Solidus clenched his hands and then turned back to the priest. The priest fell back against the altar in fear as lightning flashed in Solidus's eyes and the air around him warped and cracked.

"It would have been better for you if you had controlled your anger. Now you have set in motion something that cannot be undone. Something only the oldest of us still understand. Now you have only time before the struggle for balance ends. Remember the words I speak, Borsa Kera Moradon, tenth High Priest of Telatia. What you started here with bloodshed will end in a way you cannot even begin to imagine, and it will determine how the world ends. You have made many deadly enemies this day, and you will not soon forget it." Without another word he pointed at Rielle and both disappeared with a sound like a thousand thunder claps.

The priest slowly pulled himself off the floor, his fear being replaced by awe and greater anger. After only moments he shouted for the man outside.

"Yes, your grace?" The man asked as he quickly stepped into the room. The priest growled.

"Gather the army and march at once. I want the gates taken by week's end!" The man hastily bowed and left the room. The priest turned back to the altar, shaking with uncertainty and rage, to make council with the demon that would call him host.

Chapter Six

Solidus removed the dagger from Rielle's back and tossed it aside. He whispered a few words and a soft light covered her wound, stopping the bleeding, but her breathing did not improve and she did not wake. Solidus stood straight and called to the soldiers around the entrance of the Great Northern Gate.

"Who is in charge here?" He asked quickly. A man in chain mail armor stepped forward. He was mostly clean shaven save for some reddish stubble on his chin, and his deep green eyes watched Solidus warily.

"I am Captain Vesth, I command these soldiers that patrol the Northern Gate." Solidus nodded.

"Good, gather some of your men and take this young woman to the command pavilion and ensure she is comfortable until I arrive to heal her. The rest of your men should pull back from the gate." The captain looked at Solidus with great distrust.

"I will not jeopardize this camp by abandoning the gate." Solidus rounded on the captain, anger in his eyes.

"I don't have time to argue with you. Pull back your men or be responsible for their deaths when I pull down the mountain to block the pass." Solidus's voice was like thunder. The captain took a step back in surprise and eventually nodded under Solidus's commanding stare. "All companies pull back to the main camp!" He yelled, turning and pointing at several others.

"You men, take the woman to the command pavilion." Solidus nodded when the captain turned back around.

"Good, now stay with her until I come to heal her. She is Rielle Lyvinius, an ambassador from Hortaal. Give her diplomatic respect." The captain saluted and then turned as the soldiers carefully put Rielle on a stretcher and then lifted her and carried her off at a double march, as the captain marched behind giving orders.

Solidus turned towards the gate and closed his eyes. His right hand was held in front of him, palm facing up, with his left hand resting carefully on top of it. Ancient words poured from his mouth as he gathered his will and inner power together. He lifted his left hand and an orb of energy formed in his right. The energy twisted and turned in every direction before collapsing in on itself to create a dense coalescence of energy at the center of the orb.

For several minutes Solidus stood chanting, energy building in his hands. The wind picked up around him, blowing sand from Telatia through the pass to tear at him. Solidus paused in his chanting.

"You cannot stop me from that distance." He mumbled.

Then he gripped the ball of energy in his right hand and threw it into the gate pass. He quickly twisted and danced as if fighting some unseen enemy and silver strings shot from his fingers to follow the orb under the gate and into the pass. With a shout, he released his clenched right hand and a roar shook through the ground, those nearby feeling a deep vibration shake them to the bone.

There was an earth shattering explosion as great pieces of rock sheared off from the wall of the mountain and were pulled inward, toward the center of the pass. Solidus continued to twist and turn, manipulating the strings in his hands. Several minutes passed before Solidus finally dropped his hands to his sides, the silver strings disappearing.

He looked at his work and nodded with satisfaction. The wall of rock that filled the Northern Pass was almost identical the one in the south-west. Giant boulders packed tightly together in an almost sheer cliff. Solidus took a deep breath to calm the rapid beat of his inner power and then turned and made his way to the command pavilion.

All along the way, soldiers stood respectfully to the side of the path. Some saluting, some simply staring in awe. Solidus swept into the command pavilion and motioned for the soldiers to leave. Once they were gone only three people remained. The army commander, a wizened old man in medic's clothing, and Captain Vesth. The medic turned to look at Solidus.

"This is a mortal wound, there is nothing that can be done for her." Solidus nodded. "Thank you, you may go." The medic harrumphed and nodded, then left the pavilion with his bag of supplies.

"I am sorry she cannot be saved." The commander stated. "I have met Ambassador Rielle on a few occasions and she is a great loss for her kingdom." Solidus shook his head.

"She can be saved, though doing so will take my body." The commander, a tall man with graying hair and wide shoulders, looked at Solidus.

"But the wound is mortal, it is a miracle she has survived this long." Solidus shook his head again.

"Not a miracle. Magic." The commander's eyes widened and Captain Vesth took a step back, touching his forehead to ward away evil.

"I am Grandmaster Solidus, The Ageless Hermit Mage." The commander's eyes widened further and he quickly bowed at the waist.

"I had no idea that you had been found. We had lost hope of you coming to our aid." Captain Vesth stiffly followed his commander's example and bowed. Solidus motioned with his hand.

"We do not have time to waste at the present. I must heal Rielle quickly. When I do my body will fade and disappear. I will no longer be able to protect her from harm. When she leaves this place, I would ask that Captain Vesth accompany her as an escort." The commander nodded immediately.

"Of course." Solidus glanced at the captain. The captain bowed again.

"It will be an honor to escort the ambassador." Solidus nodded.

"It will be a few days at least. Even with my healing, it will be sometime before she recovers. Now I must act. Remember what I have said." The Commander nodded and Solidus stepped to Rielle's side.

He placed one hand on her forehead and the other over her stomach, finding the faint pulse of her inner power. Slowly he chanted, speaking in a language that caused those who heard it to tremble. Solidus raised his eyes as if speaking to someone across the bed from Rielle. Slowly, at first, and then faster, a glow began to cover Rielle. Light poured from her in rivers and waterfalls, and the more the glow grew in brightness, the more translucent Solidus became. The glow continued to build until it was blinding and the commander and the captain were forced to turn away. Slowly the glow faded back to nothing and the two men were able to turn back and look.

Rielle lay alone on the bed, breathing evenly and stably. On the floor beside the bed lay a cloak, a bow, and a sword. The commander shook himself and looked up at Captain Vesth.

"Get some men and set up a diplomatic tent for the ambassador. Then carry her, bed and all, to her tent and post a guard in case she wakes." Captain Vesth saluted.

"Yes commander." He left the tent and could be heard shouting orders. The commander turned back to look at Rielle again.

"What now? What do we do now that the Hermit Mage is gone?"

* * *

Rielle woke with a throbbing pain in the center of her back. She laid there, trying to remember what had happened, but was unable to think through the haze. Trying to sit up only made things worse, and she was forced to lay back with a groan.

Immediately she heard someone enter the tent in which she was laying. She tried to look over but could only make out a vague image of a soldier in chain mail.

"Ambassador, it is good to see you are finally awake." The soldier said. Rielle tried to speak but nothing came out the first time. She carefully cleared her throat, causing another sharp pain in her back, and tried again.

"Where am I?" The soldier waved his hand behind him.

"You are at what is left of the camp near the Great Northern Gate." Rielle thought back carefully and then spoke again.

"How did I get here?" The soldier suddenly seemed nervous.

"I will summon the Commander and Captain Vesth. They will be able to explain everything to you." Rielle nodded slowly and managed to wave her hand dismissively. The soldier quickly saluted and left the tent. Rielle heard words exchanged outside and then footsteps running into the distance. Eventually she gave up trying to sit and just laid on her bed, examining what she could of the room.

The tent she was in was large and well furnished, with a table and chairs along with a larger, padded chair at the head of the table. It was almost identical to many diplomatic tents she had stayed in during discussions on neutral ground. The tent itself was nothing to get excited over. A simple canvas tent, soaked in oil to make it waterproof, with a pole in the center and flaps on the ceiling to let the light in.

Rielle sighed, and then caught her breath as the pain in her back returned. She did not have to wait long before two men entered her tent, each saluting and then bowing once before pulling a chair over next to her bed.

"It is good to see you awake Ambassador Rielle." Said one soldier in plate armor with gold leafing across his shoulder.

"Commander Thereon of Gentry, I am pleased to see you are well." The commander half bowed in his seat.

"Thank you, but it is you who I am pleased to see well. For a while we almost didn't think you were going to make it." Rielle's eyebrows drew together.

"What happened, I cannot piece together the memories." The commander coughed once uncomfortably.

"Well, I don't know the whole story, just since you arrived here." Rielle's eyes widened and her shock grew as the commander told her of how she and Solidus had appeared out of thin air before the gate with a sound like thunder. She had been mortally wounded with a knife in the back, the commander said. Solidus had placed a spell on her to keep her alive and ordered her to be brought to the commander's pavilion and then proceeded to use his unimaginable powers to destroy the Northern Gate.

Rielle noticed that every time the commander mentioned magic, the captain that stood just behind and to one side of him made a sign to ward away evil. The commander continued and told how the camp medic had said there was no way to save Rielle, but Solidus had sacrificed his own body to heal hers.

Rielle laid numbly on the bed, using all of her will power to avoid showing any emotion at all, though tears welled up in her eyes.

"What is to happen now, commander?" She asked. The commander shrugged his shoulders.

"I am not certain. Master Solidus said you would need to be escorted by Captain Vesth when you left." He motioned to the man behind him, who nodded stiffly. "But when and where you would go I do not know. When Master Solidus healed you, his body disappeared, leaving only his cloak and his sword and his bow." Rielle nodded carefully.

"How long have I been asleep?"

"A full week." Captain Vesth finally spoke, his voice hard, but oddly sympathetic. Rielle nodded again.

"Then we must hurry. What time of day is it?"

"Early morning." The commander answered. "Half the camp is not even awake yet." Rielle thought silently to herself for a few moments.

"We should leave by this afternoon."

"Are you sure you will be able to travel so soon?" The commander asked. Rielle nodded. "I have no choice. I must speak with the king in Serriana and then sail back to Hortaal and speak with the High King there. If you will provide me with a horse, I do not think I will find it hard to travel the distance." The commander nodded and then turned to Captain Vesth. "Prepare your horse and another for the ambassador. If you ride out at a steady pace you should reach Serriana in two days. Accompany her on the ship to Hortaal and then your charge will be done and you may return here." The captain saluted without a word and then bowed to Rielle before leaving the tent. The commander sighed.

"Most of the men in camp were shook up by your arrival with Master Solidus. Most believe that everything is well because you are an ambassador from our allies in Hortaal, and Solidus healed you from a mortal wound. But unfortunately there are some, like Captain Vesth, who believe that no matter how it is used, Magic is a vile and evil practice." Rielle sighed, this time the pain was not enough to cause her breath to catch.

"Evil is sealed in the Mercury mountains. If magic was evil, it would have been sealed there as well. Solidus taught me that." The commander nodded.

"If my men could be convinced of that I would not be so worried." Rielle turned her head and looked at the commander.

"You think Captain Vesth may try something?" The commander quickly shook his head. "Not Vesth, no. He is fiercely loyal and will follow every order without question. Even if he does not like magic, he will endure being near it to follow his orders, for a time at least. It is the others that worry me. Not all of them are as disciplined and principled as Vesth." Rielle tried to sit up again. This time she succeeded, though a groan still escaped her lips. The commander placed a hand on her shoulder to steady her then stood and walked to the tent entrance.

"I will send someone with food and drink for you. And the medic to ensure you are alright before you head out." Rielle nodded.

"Could you also have Solidus's things brought to me?" She asked. "I wish to keep them." The commander bowed.

"Of course." He turned and swept through the tent flap and was gone. Rielle slowly, using the chairs as support, managed to drag herself over to the large padded chair and sit down, reclining back in its soft support. A soldier came in carrying a large tray of food and a pitcher of water. He placed it on the table with a bow and then turned to go. Before he got halfway to the door, however, he stopped and turned back. Rielle read his face immediately.

"He is disgusted with me." She thought to herself.

"I was raised as a good upstanding lad." The soldier said. "Always taught the difference between right and wrong."

"He is going to attack me." She realized. *"What can I do? I am too weak to run, and if I call for help he will kill me before help arrives."*

"I was always taught that the purge was necessary to keep us all alive." The soldier continued. "Magic drives all its users mad, and all those it is used on become an infectious disease that kills and maims." Solidus's words flowed back to Rielle. *If you are in a situation you have no experience in, you must assess the situation. If you are in harm's way, you must protect yourself accordingly.*

"Well, I am definitely in harm's way." Rielle quickly looked for her inner power.

"By all rights, miss ambassador, you should be dead a long time ago. But the man used magic to keep you alive." The soldier quickly made the sign to ward off evil. Rielle started to will her power to beat faster.

"The man used his evil powers to bring you back to life." The soldier reached down to his side and took hold of his sword handle. Rielle directed the power to her arms and let it start to build.

"Solidus was not an evil man. He was trying to save all of us." The soldier shook his head.

"If you think that way then obviously the evil has started to effect you." He drew his sword and took a step towards Rielle.

"Please don't make me hurt you." Rielle said, almost begging. The soldier smiled sadly. "You can barely keep yourself upright in that chair miss ambassador, I don't think you will be hurting anyone." Rielle found that she was slouching badly. *As your energy builds stand straight and tall, as if in the presence of royalty.* Solidus's instructions floated back to her from her memories. She forced herself to sit up straight. The soldier's sad smile turned into a frown. "At least you will die with dignity." He said, then he leapt at her, sword raised above his head. Rielle's anger boiled within her and a single shout escaped her lips.

"No!" The image of her shield filled with power and a shining purple barrier leapt up around her. The soldier crashed into the shield and was flung backwards onto the floor. Rielle felt the pressure in front of her grow as the soldier was thrown and the strain made her lose her shield. She laid back in her chair, panting, almost sobbing with the pain in her back. The soldier quickly stood and stared at Rielle with a mixture of fear and disgust.

The soldier took a step as if to attack again, but a hand grabbed his sword arm and pulled him off balance. Captain Vesth stepped into the tent and struck the soldier hard, breaking his nose. The soldier dropped to the floor again, clutching at his nose with his empty hand as crimson blood gushed from him. Captain Vesth stepped between Rielle and the soldier.

"Why do you attack the ambassador? Are you trying to

start a war with Hortaal?" Captain Vesth asked. The soldier stood.

"Captain, she has been touched by magic and is tainted. We are all in danger if she is allowed to live." The Captain stood his ground.

"The commander ordered that she would be protected as long as she is in this camp. Are you going to disobey orders soldier?" The soldier looked between Captain Vesth and Rielle. The he pointed his sword at Rielle

"But she used magic too Captain!" Captain Vesth looked over his shoulder at Rielle with an unreadable expression.

"*Will he attack me as well, now that he knows?*" The captain turned back to the soldier. "That is irrelevant. Our orders say we protect her, and protect her we shall." The soldier stammered and didn't look as if he would back down.

"Or would you rather face me instead soldier." Vesth carefully laid a single hand on the curved sword at his side. The soldier trembled for several moments before his sword dropped to the floor.

"No, Captain, I would not." Vesth nodded and his hand left his sword.

"Good." The Captain clapped once and two guards came in from outside. "Take him to Commander Thereon. Await my arrival before the commander places judgment." The two guards saluted then took the soldier by the arms and led him from the tent. Vesth turned around and looked at Rielle with that same unreadable expression. Rielle met his gaze evenly.

"What will you do, now that you know, Captain Vesth? Solidus began training me before he... died." It was still difficult for Rielle to admit. "All I can do is raise a shield around me that can protect me from physical harm. I will not hold it against you if you wish to let another be my escort." Vesth watched her carefully for several moments before speaking.

"Master Solidus asked for me to protect you by name. As much as I despise magic, I would not defy his orders, even in death." Rielle thought she almost saw a flash of fear and respect play across his face. "And Commander Thereon has also commanded that I act as your escort. I will fulfill my orders as they have been given." Vesth turned back towards the door. "The horses are ready. Eat your fill ambassador, we will leave as soon as you are able." Without waiting for a response, he marched out of the door. Rielle let out a deep breath she had been holding.

"I think I am going to have to work on that one." She thought to herself. *"Befriending him would be much better than simply making him follow orders."* Satisfied that she had, at least temporarily, escape danger, Rielle settled in her chair and began to eat from the tray that had been brought for her.

8

Chapter Seven

Rielle sat atop her horse, trying not to cringe at every step of the horses hooves, carefully inspecting the soldier that rode beside her. Besides his reddish brown hair, and green eyes, Captain Vesth really had no defining features. He stared straight ahead as if he did not notice Rielle's inspection. He had removed his usual chain mail and now wore a simple tunic with Gentry's insignia on one shoulder, a gull in flight. But despite the change in clothing, his sword still hung carefully at his side. Rielle could not help but brush the sword hanging at her own side. She now wore Solidus's cloak and sword, taking some small comfort in its closeness. Despite herself, she had grown a little attached to the ageless hermit. Though she could not use either the bow, or the sword, it helped to have them close.

"*Then again,*" She thought. "*Maybe I can get Captain Vesth to teach me how to use the sword.*"

"*That could be a very good idea.*" Solidus's voice sounded inside her head and Rielle nearly toppled off her horse.

"Are you well ambassador?" Vesth asked from his mount. Rielle nodded.

"Just a wave of dizziness." She warily tried to look into her own mind.

"*Solidus?*" She thought. Several seconds passed.

"*Did you expect someone else?*" He answered in her mind. She blinked once and was glad that she rode a pace behind Vesth so he would not see the confusion plain on her face. "*I am here because my body was taken to heal yours. The balance had to remain. One body brought back to life, the other ends in death.*" Rielle thought carefully over her next words.

"*You are inside my head?*" She almost felt Solidus shuffle around in the back of her mind. "*Kind of. It is difficult to explain. Essentially we are occupying the same space, your body and mine. Working together to keep your body alive.*" Rielle nodded.

"*That is why my wound hasn't begun to heal.*" She somehow felt Solidus nod.

"*Yes, the wound will remain, but it will no longer threaten your life. Other injuries may do so, however, so don't get reckless. I can do only so much from inside you to protect you.*" Rielle nodded again.

"*Could you not have said something before? Something to help me when I was attacked back at the camp?*"

"*I did.*" Solidus replied. "*I brought the memories of what I had taught you to the surface so you could protect yourself. I could have taken over your body and protected you that way, but then others would know I am not entirely gone.*"

"Why would that matter?" Rielle asked, forgetting herself and speaking aloud.

"Why would what matter, ambassador?" Vesth asked, not turning to look at her.

"Sorry, I was thinking out loud." She apologized. Vesth gave a simple nod in response. "*Why would that matter?*" Rielle tried again. She could almost envision Solidus standing there with his patient smile.

"*No matter how much they try to contain it, the secret of my 'death' will get out. Most won't believe it, but our enemies will. In that case I can stay here, and secretly direct you, so you may stop the high priest before the Blood Moon Cycle.*" Rielle nodded her understanding. "*Remember to ask him to teach you.*" Solidus said, and then was silent. Rielle looked up at Vesth again.

"Would you teach me to use the sword?" She asked. This time Vesth did glance back at her.

"Why would you need such a skill, ambassador?" Rielle sighed.

"First, you do not need to keep calling me ambassador. My name is Rielle. Our enemies could be anywhere and it might even be best if you did not call me by my title while we are near anyone. I want this journey to be as low profile as possible." Vesth nodded.

"As you command, Rielle." He tested the name. Rielle shook her head but continued. "Second, as skilled as I am sure you are, protecting me will be much easier if I can also protect myself."

"Why not just use your magic?" Vesth asked, contempt sneaking into his voice. Rielle carefully checked her anger.

"First, it takes time and energy to create a shield. Second, Solidus taught me that it is much better to do things with your own hands if you can, rather than use magic. Magic is mechanical, working with your hands has meaning." She could feel Solidus in the back of her mind, grinning. Vesth turned and gave her a strange look. When he turned back around he spoke. "Perhaps, when we stop for the night, I will teach you." Rielle nodded,

"Thank you, captain." She received a quiet grunt in reply.

"*That was the first step in convincing him I am a friend.*" She felt Solidus's nod of approval. The rest of the evening's ride was essentially silent. The only words spoken between them were from Vesth to Rielle, to ensure she was well and could keep the pace he had set.

When night came, Vesth chose a place to camp between two low lying hills that kept them out of the wind and out of sight of the road. The captain set up a small tent for Rielle to sleep in and then gathered wood enough for a small fire. When they had settled down, the fire was started, and a small meal had been cooked and eaten, Vesth looked across the fire to Rielle. "Are you feeling well enough to learn to use your sword, miss Rielle." Rielle stopped herself from sighing. No matter how much she tried, she could not get him to stop using the word 'miss' before her name.

"I am well enough." He nodded and stood, Rielle following his example with a grimace. "*The pain will eventually fade away.*" Solidus told her within her mind.

"*I hope so.*" She replied. Rielle removed Solidus's cloak and stepped away from the fire to join Vesth.

"Draw your sword and hold it in both hands." He told her. Rielle did as she was told and carefully slid the curved steel blade from its scabbard. She held it in front of her with both hands tightly together. Vesth shook his head and stepped to her side.

"Keep your hands slightly apart and the second knuckle of your first fingers pointed forward." He slid her hands into the position he had described and Rielle was surprised to find that, for a soldier, Vesth had exceptionally soft hands.

As Vesth fixed her hand position he noticed a small mark at the base of the blade. His hands froze for a fraction of a second and then he stepped back again.

"Good, now hold your sword pointed straight in front of you, as if at an enemies eyes, and keep the base of your sword a fist's length from your naval." Rielle did as she was told, but carefully watched Vesth. She had noticed his pause.

"This is your basic position for holding your sword. When we practice, this is always how you will begin." Rielle nodded and noticed that Vesth's eyes drifted to her blade again. "What draws your eyes and causes you pause?" She asked him. His eyes snapped back to her face as if he had not been looking at the blade. She stared him down, and eventually he relented.

"The mark at the base of your blade." Rielle looked at the sword in her hands. At the base of the blade, etched into the metal, was a simple depiction of a dragon in flight.

"It is a dragon." She stated. Vesth nodded.

"A dragon is the mark of a master swordsman. A dragon curled up is the mark of a master who has just proven his abilities." Vesth drew his own sword and tilted the blade so Rielle could see the dragon, rearing up on its hind legs, etched on his sword.

"The rearing dragon is a veteran master. But the flying

dragon," He returned his sword to its scabbard and openly stared at Rielle's sword. "The flying dragon is supposed to be the mark of a master unsurpassed by any other. I have never before seen any swordsman with a flying dragon on their blade."

"That is because there are very few of us. May I speak with him directly?" Solidus asked Rielle. Rielle nodded and then gasped as she felt herself drawn back into her own mind. She could still see through her eyes, and hear everything around her, but she could not move her body or speak. Vesth took a step back in surprise as the bright blue in Rielle's eyes drained away and was replaced by a clear silver.

"Do not be worried Captain Vesth, It is Solidus that speaks with you now." Solidus's voice overlaid Rielle's and created a strange, quiet harmony. Vesth stared in obvious shock. "Master Solidus?" Rielle felt her head shake.

"I think Rielle has made it quite obvious that titles are not needed on this journey." Vesth nodded carefully.

"How is it possible you are here?" He asked. Solidus smiled and replied.

"My body was taken to heal Rielle, but my mind rests carefully in the recesses of hers. I can manifest when I must, but I would prefer that no one knows that I am still alive, in a manner of speaking." Vesth nodded carefully again.

"Why do you manifest yourself now?" He asked shakily. Solidus chuckled, a strange feeling to Rielle.

"You are shocked by the dragon mark on my sword." Solidus stated. "It was placed there many years ago, when I still lived in High King Hortaal's court." Vesth blinked in surprise and Solidus laughed.

"I am much older than that, Vesth, become accustomed to it. That is one reason my skill has grown to fill that mark." Rielle felt herself tap the mark on the side of the blade in her hand. Vesth just stared at the sword, nodding slowly.

"Would you like to spar? It will be easier to understand if you experience it." Vesth looked at Rielle/Solidus suspiciously. Solidus smiled knowingly. "There will be no magic involved. Just skill, pure and simple. I think Rielle has already told you that I do not believe in doing something with magic that can be done with your own hands." Most of Vesth's suspicions disappeared and he nodded.

"It would be an honor to spar with you, Master Solidus." Solidus returned his sword to his scabbard.

"You may begin when you wish." Solidus stated. "My sword will leave it's scabbard when it becomes necessary." Rielle suddenly felt extremely tense. She would be fighting a master swordsman and she had only just learned to hold a sword.

All will be well. Solidus told her. Vesth drew his sword and stood in the stance that he had taught Rielle. Rielle noted that it was much better than she had managed.

Before Rielle could comprehend what was happening, Vesth struck and Solidus's sword left it's scabbard to intercept the incoming blade. Vesth's sword was deflected, but he quickly recovered and struck again. Rielle would have been afraid of the skill Vesth fought with if she had not been in shock at the speed with which he and Solidus traded blows.

The fight lasted only a few seconds. In the end, Solidus disarmed Vesth and returned his sword to his scabbard in a single, smooth movement. Vesth stared at his hands in shock and then back up at Rielle/Solidus.

"You are an Iai Master." He said quietly. Rielle felt herself nod.

"I trained to be so for a great many years. Now I must rest. Controlling Rielle's body is a difficult task and I grow tired. For now, teach her the forms and let her practice. She will learn quickly, but it will take a long time before she is ready to fight any sort of battle." Vesth nodded with a short bow that was, Rielle noticed, not as stiff as it had been. Then Rielle felt herself pulled back to the front of her mind and she shook herself as her eyes turned blue again.

"You are amazing." She told Vesth, finding that Solidus's voice was no longer mixing with her own. Vesth retrieved his sword and returned it to its scabbard.

"I am proficient. But I am obviously far from amazing." Rielle searched for an argument to better his mood.

"Solidus has a head start on you by a very long time. I am sure that if you were as old as he is, you would be equally skilled, if not more so." Vesth shrugged and waved her off.

"Perhaps, But I am not as old as he, and will not likely live to be as old. My skill will never match his."

"*It doesn't need to.*" Solidus told Rielle.

"It doesn't need to." Rielle told Vesth, and he looked at her with questioning eyes.

"You don't need to match Solidus, or even come close for that matter." Rielle insisted. "He is our ally, not our enemy. You need only be stronger than your enemy." Vesth turned his eyes to the ground and Rielle saw the unhappiness in his face lessen. After a few moments he straightened and turned back to Rielle.

"Draw your sword, we have a lot to do." Rielle nodded with a smile and drew Solidus's sword.

* * *

Rielle sat down tiredly next to the fire. Vesth had drilled her on multiple forms and sword movements until she could repeat each of them from memory. Solidus had given silent instruction when it was necessary, but otherwise kept to himself and allowed Rielle to learn.

She tried to reach around and rub the wound on her back, which had begun to ache, but could not reach. Eventually she gave up and simply tried to find a comfortable position. Vesth added wood to the fire.

"You learn very quickly miss Rielle." Vesth commented. "I have known soldiers that took days to memorize the forms you just learned." Rielle would have shrugged, but didn't dare try. "Being an ambassador requires a good memory. Forgetting a name or a custom can be disastrous during negotiations." Vesth nodded and continued to stoke the fire. There was silence for many minutes before Rielle spoke again.

"What is an Iai Master?" She asked. Vesth glanced up from the fire. Rielle painfully half shrugged in an apparent lack of interest. "I remember you calling Solidus an Iai Master. What is it?" Vesth carefully took the stick he had been using to prod coals and set it aside before looking back at Rielle.

"Iai is a special set of sword forms. Very secret and difficult to learn. Few learn the technique and it is difficult to implement in battle." Rielle leaned forward to show she was listening.

"Why is it so difficult?" Vesth stared into the fire.

"The basic idea of Iai is not to draw your sword, or even

move, until the last moment. Your sword and sword arm remains still and idle until it must be put into action. It is almost impossible to read Iai because you do not telescope your movements to your enemy. They do not know what you are going to do until you do it. But it requires a great deal of patients, dexterity, and timing. If you are off in any of those, you could end up dead before you realize your sword should have moved." Rielle's eyes were wide.

"Do you know Iai?" Vesth nodded.

"Yes, but I use it only to train. I would not dare use it in battle. I do not want to worry about if I will make that one fatal mistake that could end the fight."

"It took me a great many years to master it, and many more after before it earned me the Flying Dragon." Solidus commented.

"Might I be able to learn it? After I first become proficient with the technique you have already taught me that is." Vesth shrugged.

"It could take years to become proficient in what you already know. Mastering the simple forms are the most effective in self defense."

"True. Simple is best." Solidus agreed.

"Wait until you are confident in your abilities, then you may speak with the High King in Hortaal. He is your governing patriarch, it is his permission you must receive to learn Iai." Rielle nodded.

"The High King and I are distant cousins. I am sure that if I can show him that I am at least fairly proficient, he will give his permission." Vesth shrugged.

"In a few years perhaps. Until then you will have to learn

what I can teach you." Rielle nodded again and then yawned. She thought she almost saw Vesth smile.

"Get some sleep miss Rielle, we ride at sunrise." Rielle nodded and almost had to crawl into the small tent. The moment her head touched the soft pillow that Commander Thereon had provided her, she was asleep. She dreamed very little and what she did dream faded into nothing when she woke in the morning. She left the tent to find Vesth with breakfast ready and the horses ready to leave.

While she ate, he quickly packed the tent and then put out the fire. When she was finished, he quickly washed her dish and packed it away as well before offering his assistance to Rielle to help her into her saddle. It was then that Rielle realized how stiff and sore her shoulders and arms were, not to mention her back. After a moment of internal debate, and despite the hurt to her pride, she accepted and she climbed into the saddle with his aid.

They set out at the same pace they had maintained the previous day, and by evening Rielle was glad to slide off of her horse. Vesth methodically set up the camp and started the fire. After a warm meal, he had Rielle stand and review her forms for what seemed like an eternity to her. She slept well again that night and, again, accepted Vesth's help in the morning to mount her horse. By late afternoon, Rielle could smell the ocean and see the great city of Serriana rising up on the horizon.

"There is a back gate that follows a stone corridor into the palace grounds." Rielle stated. "I think it would be best if we entered the city though there." Vesth nodded and nudged his mount to a greater pace. Rielle did not complain, but was glad to get down when they reached the small gate to the far east of the city. As she walked the rest of the distance to the gate, Rielle reached into a small pouch at her side and removed a signet ring which she placed on her right hand.

Two guards, in grey armor, stood before the small gate, nearly filling it's area. Both bowed and stepped aside when Rielle showed them her ring and the gate was opened. Now Rielle led the way down a short ramp and along a stone corridor, wide enough for a cart but only as high as a horse and rider. The corridor led on for several hundred feet before another short ramp led up into sunlight on a courtyard covered in spars tan grass. Two stablemen met them there and took their horses. Rielle only paused for a moment to take Solidus's bow from where it had been tied to her saddle before she started off towards the grey marble palace.

Halfway Vesth excused himself, saying he had to meet with someone in the city first, before they sailed for Hortaal. Rielle vaguely waved him off and continued through the palace's front door and into a grand hall.

Rielle announced herself and showed her ring to a servant boy, who then led her through the dark palace corridors until they came to a tall door inlaid with gold. Rielle waited patiently outside while the servant announced her, making sure her hair was in place and her cloak was swept aside to ensure that Solidus's sword was not covered. The servant returned and waved her through.

She thanked the boy and then walked through the doors and into a small meeting hall with a high-backed throne on a raised dais at the far end. To either side of the throne stood an advisor to the king. On the throne itself sat a large man with green eyes, graying red hair, and a full beard. He had large arms and legs and thickly calloused hands from many years of towing lines and piloting the great sailing ships that were the pride of the Gentry navy. Rielle bowed deeply to the man then straightened.

"Greetings King Yisu. May fair winds be at your back." The king smiled down at Rielle. "Greetings Ambassador Rielle Lyvinius. What brings you to my court?" Rielle pouted and was satisfied to see the king lean forward in anticipation of her words. She told him the story of how she had met Solidus and brought him back to assist them. She omitted the parts of the story about her mage potential and the old stories Solidus had told her.

The king's eyes widened when she told of the destruction of the great gates and of the High Priest of Telatia's plan to attack during the Blood Moon Cycle. She told of her injury and how Solidus had healed her at the expense of his body, leaving out that he was inside her now. She noticed one of the advisors make a sign to ward off evil. When she told the king of the soldier who had tried to kill her, the king's face filled with outrage.

"I swear he will be severely punished!" He cried. Rielle hid a smile.

"I thank you, King Yisu, But Commander Thereon has already decided his punishment." The king sat back in his throne.

"Excellent, Thereon is a good man. He will make sure the traitor is dealt with." Rielle continued.

"I came here to warn you of the coming Blood Moon Cycle." She stated. "Fighting the enemy on that night would only make them stronger. Master Solidus suggested that every city be prepared for siege and be locked up and carefully guarded on that night to reduce casualties. Once it is over, the enemy will be spread thin and can be wiped out." The king nodded, deep in thought.

"So you did manage to find The Hermit Mage." He said. Rielle nodded.

"Yes, it seems the old texts in your library were correct." The advisor to the king's left spoke.

"What led you to believe that this, Solidus, truly was the Hermit Mage?" Rielle looked at him with a questioning glance.

"Were you not listening when I told of the Gate's destruction? Hundreds of soldiers witnessed it." The advisor nodded.

"I was listening, but the Mercury Mountains are fabled to hold great evils. How do you know that what you brought with you was not just some evil being with magical powers?" Rielle could feel Solidus's amusement in the back of her mind.

"Would an evil creature have chosen to help us? Would an evil creature sacrifice itself to heal me from a mortal wound? If this is not enough for you, I do have one small piece of evidence that I am sure you will be unable to deny." The king's eyebrows rose.

"What is the evidence you carry?" He asked with interest. Both advisors nodded. Rielle smiled innocently and placed one hand on Solidus's sword. The advisor on the king's right drew a rapier with lightning speed and leveled it at Rielle. The king swatted the flat of his advisor's blade, batting it aside.

"She is no swordsman, Genru, she does not pose a threat in any way." The advisor harrumphed and lowered his blade, but he did not return it to its scabbard. Rielle removed Solidus's sword from its scabbard and held the blade in her empty hand, presenting it to the king. The king's eyes grew wide, Genru quickly deposited his rapier back in its scabbard, and the advisor on the king's left made a quiet surprised sound.

"The flying dragon." The king marveled. "The teacher of the High King, Hortaal Lyvinius, was the last said to have a blade with the flying dragon etched in its surface. At least, the last one who was documented." Rielle nodded and sheathed the sword.

"Master Solidus was the teacher of High King Hortaal. He truly was the Ageless Hermit Mage. When you looked into his eyes you could see the depth of his age and knowledge and power."

"*Careful.*" Solidus cautioned. "*My eyes were so for a reason. It is, perhaps, not wise to get too free with the information. It was ok here, but in other places there could be those who carefully listen for descriptions such as that.*" Rielle resisted the urge to nod.

"I think there cannot be doubt as to who Master Solidus was." Rielle finished. The king nodded.

"I agree. And if what you say is true, I think it would be best if you leave immediately to relay the news to the High King in Hortaal." Rielle nodded.

"It is my wish that you would lend me the services of a ship to take me to Hortaal." The king slapped his hand down on the arm of his throne.

"Done! I will send an entire fleet with you." The advisor on the King's left opened his mouth to complain, but Rielle quickly spoke first.

"I thank you, King Yisu, But that will not be necessary.

Our enemy may still be looking for me and our best chance of making it to Hortaal in one piece is to take only a small, fast ship and travel without escort. No one will bother with a small ship that is not guarded. Nothing of value could be on board a Gentry ship that has no escort." The king scratched his chin and gradually nodded.

"Perhaps you are right. I will have my finest captain and crew ready to sail within the hour." The king stood and Rielle bowed.

"Thank you, your majesty. We will leave as soon as we can, but I must wait for the one who escorted me here. He has sworn to protect me until I am conducted directly to High King Morien Toriel, by order of Commander Thereon." The king nodded and directed Rielle to the door.

"If Thereon recommended him, I trust him to protect you. Your ship will leave when both of you have boarded." Rielle bowed again and left the throne room, ready to head down to the docks and inspect the ship that would carry them to Hortaal.

9

Chapter Eight

Vesth stepped down onto the dock and walked towards the single mast ship that was moored there. Sailors scrambled across the deck, packing supplies and towing lines, preparing the ship to sail.

Rielle stood on the dock, overseeing the preparations. Supplies were carried and errands run at her command. Vesth could see the ship's captain running back and forth across the deck, shouting orders as Rielle gave them, trying to maintain at least the semblance of control over his own men. Vesth would have grinned if, at that moment, he had not caught Rielle's eye.

"It is about time you arrived." She chastised him. "We are almost ready to set sail." Vesth half bowed.

"We were unprepared for a longer journey than we had already made. There were supplies I needed to gather that King Yisu could not have provided." Rielle got a strange look on her face, as if she were silently talking to herself, then nodded.

"Very well."

"We are ready to set sail!" The captain yelled to no one in particular. The sailors remaining on the dock hurried up the plank and onto the ship. Vesth motioned for Rielle to board first and then followed. The crew quickly hauled the plank aboard and cut the lines, allowing the ship to drift out into the open sea.

The first day was uneventful as the ship sailed smoothly over the water. Vesth made Rielle practice her sword forms for several hours, telling her that the unstable footing caused by the motion of the ship would help her learn how to handle unpredictable terrain.

The second day started out just as smooth and uneventful. It was not long, however, before Rielle found Vesth and dragged him to the rear of the ship and whispered to him so that she would not be overheard.

"Solidus says that a powerful storm is growing against us. We need to land until it passes or the ship will never make it out in one piece." Vesth quickly glanced around to make sure no one was near.

"Are you certain, miss Rielle? The sky is calm and it is not the season for storms." Rielle nodded.

"Yes. If we don't land soon, the ship will break apart and we will all drown." Vesth shook his head.

"Even if the captain could be persuaded that there would be a storm, the coast is many leagues away. And most of the coast between Gentry and Hortaal is blocked by the cliffs of the Serpents Tongue mountains, there is no place to land." Rielle closed her eyes in thought and nodded.

"We are near the Island Temple of Alenon." Vesth's eyes grew wide and he made a sign to ward off evil.

"The Island Temple is a forbidden place. Any who land there are never seen again." Rielle sat still for a moment then nodded again.

"Solidus says that as long as we only dock there, and do not try to leave the ship or enter the temple, we will be safe from harm. And the storm cannot reach there." Rielle opened her eyes and noticed Vesth's skeptical look. "We have no other choice." She told him. Then, as if to emphasize her words, the rumble of thunder sounded in the distance.

Vesth's face set into hard lines and he nodded. He stood quickly and went in search of the captain. Moments later the captain scrambled up the stairs from below deck, followed quickly by Vesth. Another crack of thunder shook the air and had most of the crew looking nervously at the sky.

"A storm should not be able to grow this quickly." The captain said as he and Vesth neared Rielle. Rielle nodded.

"Indeed it should not captain. But the fact remains that it is building quickly and if we do not land somewhere your ship will not survive it." The captain shook his head.

"We cannot make landfall before we get hit. It is much too far."

"We can make it to the Island Temple." Vesth stated emotionlessly. The captain quickly made a sign to ward off evil.

"If we land at the Island Temple, none of us will ever be heard from again." Rielle shook her head.

"We will be fine as long as we only land and do not leave the ship. I have studied this place and only those intent on entering the temple have chosen to land there. We land there out of necessity and will not be harmed if we do not try to enter the temple." The captain was still shaking his head before another crack of thunder, this time much closer and louder, sounded around them.

"We have no other choice captain. We either risk our lives there with a chance that we survive, or we sit here and we all die." The captain made another sign to ward away evil and then turned to his crew and started shouting orders.

"Turn starboard! Head west!" He ran to the helm without waiting for anyone to follow his order and spun the ship into a sharp right turn. More orders were shouted and the crew leapt into action.

By the time they could finally see the glittering white temple on top of its low island, lightning was flashing over their heads and rain poured down around them. Rielle clung to the mast to avoid getting thrown overboard by giant waves that washed over the deck and crew. The ship groaned in protest, and it seemed that they would break apart before they reached the temple.

However, when they came within a few hundred feet of the shore, the weather suddenly ceased. The air was calm, the sun shone and no lightning or thunder split the sky. Behind them, Rielle could see a definite line where the storm came to a stop all the way around the island at an exact distance from the temple. As they approached the island, they found that the beach dropped off sharply into the sea and they were able to glide the ship almost within touching distance of the white sand. The crew nervously came in next to the shore and dropped the anchor. Everyone was silent as they stood anxiously, unsure of what to do.

Vesth and the captain stood to one side, keeping the crew under a tight rein with their eyes. Rielle stood a little apart with her eyes closed, conversing with Solidus. It was several minutes later that Rielle finally looked up.

"Vesth and I must leave the ship." She told the captain, her voice seemingly loud in the silence. Vesth looked at her in shock and the captain gave her a look that said she was crazy. She sighed and pulled Vesth a little ways away.

"Solidus says there is a man in the temple who we must petition to stay here for very long. This storm is likely to last long into the night." She whispered almost inaudibly so as not to be heard by anyone. Vesth nodded reluctantly and turned back to the captain.

"We have reason to believe that there may be a limit to the time we can stay here safely. If the ambassador and I make contact with the temple, we may be able to bargain for a greater period of safety. At least until the storm passes, which may take a very long time." The captain nodded to Vesth.

"Very well, but if the storm passes and you have not returned, we will leave this place without you." Vesth nodded once and turned back to Rielle. The plank was carefully lowered onto the white sand of the beach and was quickly hauled back once Vesth and Rielle were off. Rielle walked confidently towards the entrance to the temple, Vesth following behind with much less confidence. The distance was much greater than he had anticipated and by the time the temple loomed over them, the ship was just a speck in the distance. They stood before two shining Ivory doors that barred the way into the temple. The doors themselves were simple and carefully crafted to show no defect in their workmanship. Rielle casually walked up to the door, as if she belonged, and knocked three times. They waited for several moments and then Rielle knocked again. This time a voice answered the knock.

"Who is it who wishes to enter the Temple of Alenon? Speak so that I may know friend from foe." Rielle cleared her throat and spoke in a voice loud enough to pass through the door.

"I am Rielle Toriel Lyvinius, ambassador and mage in training. I am the student of..." Rielle paused for a moment and then nodded before continuing. "I am the student of Grandmaster Silver Mage, Pravin Solidus. I have traveled here with my escort." Rielle motioned for Vesth to introduce himself. Vesth looked at the door unsurely.

"I am Captain Vesth Dagda, a soldier of Gentry sworn to protect Rielle." Rielle almost smiled when Vesth did not add any titles to her name. They waited for several seconds before the voice came again.

"Speak my name, student of Solidus, that I may know you are the student of the Ageless Hermit." Rielle nodded and spoke again.

"You are Shield Archmage Siguard Agamemnon, guardian and High Priest of the Temple of Alenon." Another few moments passed in silence. Then there was a soft hum as the doors to the temple split apart and swung open.

"You may enter the temple." Came the voice again. Rielle motioned for Vesth to follow and stepped carefully through the doors. Rielle found that the inside of the Temple of Alenon was exactly the opposite as the Temple in Tyr-Anon. It was white and well lit, and the feeling in the air was one of peace and tranquility, not darkness and corruption. Rielle marveled at the beauty of the white, seemingly delicate, stone that vaulted up in pillars to the high ceiling and spread out in graceful arches that caught the sound of their every step and echoed it around them a thousand times.

They walked through a long corridor of the graceful pillars and came to another set of ivory doors. As they drew near, the doors swung open and admitted them. They entered the room and Rielle had a sudden flash of déjà vu. They entered a large room that was sparsely decorated, with magic circles engraved on the floor. At the other end was an altar of white stone that was carved so expertly that it seemed the stone had formed that way on its own naturally. Before the altar stood a man in a long white robe with brilliant silver hair.

"It has been long since people have come to the temple without the desire to plunder it." The man said, as he turned to face them. His face was round and kind, though lined with age, and his eyes were a bright blue. "Welcome, Student of Solidus. It has been a great many years since he has taught anyone. What brought him to you?" Rielle told their story from beginning to end, leaving out only that Solidus was in her mind. The man listened patiently, nodding once in a while, and thought about it silently.

"You are welcome to stay near the temple until the storm passes." The man said finally. "As long as no one tries to harm the temple or the grounds. I am the High Priest of Alenon, Agamemnon." Rielle bowed and Vesth followed suit.

"We thank you for your hospitality." Rielle said. The priest nodded.

"And you are welcome to it." Rielle made a strange face and then she nodded, gasping as her eyes turned from blue to silver. Vesth shuddered. He hadn't liked it the first time

Solidus had taken control of Rielle's body, and he wasn't so sure he liked it any more this time.

"Greetings to you Agamemnon." Solidus said, his voice layering over Rielle's. The high priest did not seem to be surprised in any way.

"This was an exceptional risk to take Solidus, that is not like you." Rielle/Solidus shrugged.

"It was, unfortunately, necessary. Though, while we are here, I would have you look to the wound that was inflicted. I am no great healer, and you may be able to do more. It would make my task much easier to perform." The high priest nodded.

"I agree, however, I think the young lady would prefer her privacy." He glanced at Vesth. Rielle/Solidus nodded.

"Indeed. Vesth, it would be wise for you to return to the ship and tell the captain that he and his crew are safe as long as they stay on the ship. Tell them that you and Rielle will be spending the night in the temple and you will return in the morning to depart. Remind them of what King Yisu may do to them if they choose to leave without you and the ambassador if it is necessary." The high priest looked over at Vesth.

"When you return to the temple, the doors will open for you and you will be conducted to a room were you may clean up and rest until dinner is served. Young Rielle will need to sleep for some time after I heal her for her body to adjust. You may also wander the temple grounds if you feel inclined. A bell will sound when dinner is ready." Vesth bowed to both of them and then turned, leaving the room quickly as the ivory doors shut behind him. Rielle/Solidus turned back to the high priest. Slowly Rielle's eyes returned to normal and she stood, uncertain of what to do. The high priest smiled kindly.

"Would you allow me to examine your wound?" Rielle nodded and removed Solidus's cloak and then paused uncertainly with her hand on the top clasp of her robe. The high priest chuckled quietly.

"You may turn and show only your wound if it bothers you to be seen otherwise. Solidus is within you of course, but both he and I have lived a very long time and seen a great many things, I am a healer after all." Rielle nodded, then turned her head slightly as if listening. After a few moments she seemed more confident and turned her back to the old priest. She unclasped her robe and let it fall just enough to show the wound between her shoulder blades.

"Please forgive me for this." The high priest stated before he carefully began touching the edges of the wound. Rielle winced more than once, and the old priest apologized each time. After several minutes went by the priest nodded.

"Solidus's healing has done its job, young Rielle. There is little left for me to do. I can close the wound, for the most part, and I can take away most of the pain, but Solidus will not be leaving you any time soon." Rielle half turned her head.

"Solidus can leave me?" The high priest shrugged.

"Yes and no. There are ways he could separate himself from you, but to do so right now would kill you. And even if your wound ever healed enough for him to leave you, it could cause much more harm than good. This exchange is more or less permanent, unless both of you wish to risk damage to yourselves. You would also need an intermediary, and I am not near so old and foolish as to be the one." Rielle opened her mouth to ask another question, but the old priest quickly raised a hand to silence her.

"It is of little consequence. As I said before, even with my healing it would be a very long time before Solidus could even attempt to leave you safely, if that time came at all. For now, I will heal you as best I can and we will worry about things like that later." Rielle closed her mouth and nodded. The high priest returned her nod.

"When I perform the healing on you, your consciousness will go to sleep to help your body heal. Solidus will take over your body and take it to a place you may rest. It will be unlike when you are awake and you will have no memory of what happens before you wake. I am telling you now so you will not worry when you wake and find yourself in a strange place." Rielle nodded and then turned her head away and closed her eyes.

The high priest placed his hands on Rielle's back, one on either side of the wound, and closed his eyes, beginning to chant in an ancient language. A glow enveloped the wound and it seemed to shrink, and the edges became less enflamed. The process took no more than a minute, but the effect was easily noticeable. Afterwards, there was a moment where Rielle started to collapse, but she quickly caught herself and tied the clasps on her robe shut again. Then she turned, her eyes a clear silver, and looked at the high priest. When he spoke this time, Solidus's voice was alone, Rielle's voice gone in her state of sleep.

"Thank you Agamemnon, her journey will be made much easier now." The old priest frowned.

"Are you sure you know what you are doing Solidus? If

your plan fails, balance could be torn apart and the demons would have what they wanted." Solidus nodded.

"I know, but If we do nothing the effect would be the same." The high priest shook his head slowly.

"Be careful, Solidus. She would not be pleased if the time is not right and you try to fulfill this prediction." Solidus nodded.

"I know, but it is a risk I have to take. Everything has fallen too precisely into place to be coincidence. Even to the placement of the thrown knife that injured the young one." Solidus tapped Rielle's shoulder for emphasis. "If I had not been watching for the predictions to begin all these years and had not watched the first few steps happen over neutral space, I would almost have thought that the demons and the High Priest Borsa were trying to force it. But the blow was out of rage, it was not planned. If it had been I would have seen it soon enough to prevent it. And the other steps taken were not by any tainted by the chaos. It is too precise to be anything but the prediction. If it is not, I think she will forgive me." The high priest sighed.

"You presume much, Solidus." Solidus shrugged.

"I am a balance mage, the last one. Presuming is what I do. The balance must remain, how it is achieved is of little matter. That is why the predictions are all different. Your predecessor taught me that, before I taught it to you when he passed on. Remember why you guard Alenon." The high priest frowned again.

"And what of you?" Solidus sighed and turned to the door.

"My duty is not to Alenon. I was charged with balance and balance must remain. When the ship sails, and we arrive on the mainland again, I will begin gathering them together. The one who comes with this young one is also part of the balance. I could order him to follow her, but the balance will be stronger if he is convinced to make the choice himself. Speak with him, before the night is through." The high priest nodded and half bowed.

"As you wish, Master Solidus." Solidus nodded and walked through the opening ivory doors.

"Goodnight, Agamemnon, this control of Rielle tires me, I must rest. You will not hear from me again before we depart. Make sure everything is in order. I do not wish to return to Alenon before I must." The high priest nodded.

"I will pass the word on to the other two. They will be in readiness before the Blood Moon rises." Solidus nodded once more and left the room, seeking a bed for Rielle, and rest for himself.

10

Chapter Nine

Vesth lay on his back in the small temple room he had been given to stay in. His stomach was full, but he had not enjoyed his meal. Before dinner, the high priest had asked to speak with him privately. Vesth was unsure of who it was that might overhear, as he had seen no other person since they had arrived, but he abliged the old man.

The high priest had sat him down in a small sitting room and asked him if he was going to accompany Rielle. Vesth had told the old priest that his duty was to see her safely to Hortaal. The high priest greeted this with a chuckle and a shake of his head.

"I did not ask what your duties were. I asked if you would be joining young Rielle. Her journey does not end in Hortaal. She must travel much further afterwards, gathering allies to fight against the Telatian High Priest. The Blood Moon Cycle grows close, and even traveling quickly with little rest, it will be difficult for her to gather them quickly enough." Vesth had turned his head to stare at his boots and remained silent. The high priest sighed.

"As much as you have seen, you should know by now that magic is not evil." Vesth's breath caught momentarily, but he kept his eyes pinned to his boots. "Do you know of Alenon?" The high priest asked. Vesth spoke without looking up.

"King Yisu's library contains books speaking of a great kingdom called Alenon, that sank into the sea." The high priest nodded.

"Alenon was once a great kingdom, populated by people who were righteous and good. They served others and healed the sick, and were considered good to all people. They served the Deity of Good, spreading their influence to all places... And they were all powerful magic users, blessed with their gift from the Deity of Good." Vesth raised his head enough to look at the high priest out of the corner of his eye. The high priest nodded.

"But they became overzealous. They came to see the rest of the world as evil and thought they should be converted to good. But if they had done such a thing, they would have thrown the world out of balance and it might have come to an end." Vesth's eyes widened marginally. The high priest nodded sadly.

"So, to maintain the balance, Alenon was thrown into the sea. Only the Great Temple of Alenon remained, along with four children of Alenon." Vesth raised his head to look fully on the priest now. The high priest nodded again, sadness causing him to look much older.

"I was the youngest, only fifteen at the time. The other three were all much older. The oldest was a master mage who relied on balance. His name... was Pravin Solidus, the Gifted One." Vesth's eyes widened fully and he fell back against his chair, hanging limply. The high priest nodded again.

"The very same Solidus who has given up his body to sustain the life of Rielle. He taught the rest of us in the ways of balance, peace, and harmony. Then each of us was given a task by our Deity. I was to remain and guard the last remaining piece of Alenon. Solidus became a hermit, and was charged with protecting balance in the world. The other two mages who were left were given tasks that sent them out into the world. We are the remaining Four of Alenon. The only ones left to protect its proud name. Our magic was gifted to us to protect and heal, for good, not evil. Cast aside your doubts, Vesth Dagda, cast aside the limiting bond of the order given you. Think of what Rielle must do, for good, now that Solidus is no longer able to freely travel the world. Think of the danger she will face, the weight of the task that has fallen to her and then decide where your true duty lies." A bell had then rang somewhere deep in the temple. The high priest stood. And opened the door for Vesth.

"Dinner is ready. Think on what I have told you. You have a long time to think it over. Over dinner, and the rest of your journey to Hortaal." Vesth had stood, bowed, and silently left the room. He had eaten mechanically during dinner, never really tasting his food, though Rielle had made a great many comments on how good it was. Now Vesth lay on his back on the comfortable bed in his room, replaying the discussion over and over in his head.

"Decide where your true duty lies." Vesth repeated to himself quietly. He tried to rationalize that magic had to be evil.

He had been taught his entire life to view it as such and to fear it. He was certain that anyone who used magic must also be evil, and that he could have no duty that required him to follow such a person. His resolve wavered when he tried to think of Rielle as evil.

He tried to make everything fit together as he had been taught. But the high priest's words had taken their effect and slowly, over the course of the night, he realized that there was no way he could convince himself that Rielle or Master Solidus were evil. He placed one hand over his heart where he could feel something resting in the place he had left it when he left Serriana. Vesth sat up slowly as the first light of day broke through the window and landed in golden pools on his bed. He quickly packed his things and left his room. Rielle was already awake with a small pack of her things sitting on the floor beside her. She stood talking with the high priest before she noticed his approach and turned.

"Did you sleep well?" She asked him. Vesth shrugged.

"It means little how I slept. We should depart immediately. The sooner we reach Hortaal the better." Rielle nodded and bid goodbye to the high priest. He bowed and bid her farewell and told her to let Solidus know he would do what was needed. She agreed she would and then turned and left through the temple's ivory doors. Vesth bowed to the high priest and made his way out the door.

As he left, he heard the old man mumble, 'Remember your duty.', and then the doors shut behind him and he was rushing down the path to catch up with Rielle. They boarded the ship and the anxious crew happily obeyed their captain's order to set sail. It took them another two days to reach a port in Hortaal where they could buy horses and make their way to the Capital City. Vesth paid an old man several pieces of silver for two horses, grumbling that he could have gotten them at half the price in Gentry. Rielle just smiled and told him it was better than walking to the capital.

"If the weather holds fair, it shouldn't take us more than a few days." Rielle told him. Vesth looked warily at the sky. Rielle shrugged, then looked around to make sure no one would over hear them. "Solidus says that whoever conjured the storm that hit us did not weave their magic in balance. It took a heavy toll on them and they won't be creating any more storms to bother us, not for a very long time." Vesth shrugged uncomfortably and kept one eye on the clouds overhead.

Their journey was the same as it had been before, back in Gentry. They set out early in the morning and did not stop until it was almost dark. When they stopped Vesth quickly, and efficiently, set up the camp and then continued to teach Rielle to use her sword.

On the second night, Vesth cut two thick branches, about the length of a sword, and gave one to Rielle. They sparred, and Vesth showed Rielle how to use each stance to block and parry and strike at an opponent. Rielle learned quickly, if she didn't, Vesth would reward her with a sound strike with his branch. He never hit hard enough to bruise, but it was hard enough to remind Rielle how not to use her weapon. Rielle slept soundly that night and woke to find Vesth already packed and ready to go.

"I don't like the feeling in these trees." He explained when she questioned his hurry. Rielle calculated the distance they had traveled already.

"We are in the thickest part of the Forest of Hortaal, apart from the Moon Witch Forest of course. Perhaps it would be wise to ride steady today and not pause if it can be helped. Hortaal is peaceful, but there are places where even the legions of Hortaal cannot reach to keep the peace. Especially now, with the war having spread our forces so thin." They rode for several hours, and each passing hour left Rielle with a tighter and tighter knot in her stomach.

"Do not hold it back." Solidus spoke to her. *"Your senses are trying to tell you something. Let your power beat and let your mind focus on what they are saying."* Rielle nodded and closed her eyes, willing her inner power to beat faster and directing her energy to the knot she felt in her stomach. Slowly the knot unwound and Rielle suddenly felt as if she could hear something *"There are voices."* She told Solidus. She almost felt Solidus nodding.

"They are trying to tell you something. Listen, and see if you can hear what they say." Rielle listened carefully to the jumble of mumbling voices for several moments before they began making sense to her.

"They are saying something about a shapeless form speaking to a dark personage. The shapeless form is saying something that is making the dark personage greedy, but bound at the same time."

"Perhaps you have the gift." Solidus said. *"And perhaps not. Time will tell."* Solidus was silent for several moments. Rielle wanted to ask Solidus what he meant by 'gift', but she knew he would likely not give her a straight answer.

"You are right about the voices. Another choice is being made

and we must move our plans ahead. Let me speak with Vesth." Rielle nodded and looked over at Vesth as he rode warily down the packed dirt road.

"Vesth? Solidus wishes to speak with you." Vesth reigned in his horse and turned in his saddle.

"What is it?" Rielle shivered and her eyes turned silver. Solidus spoke.

"Events are unfolding that will require us to move sooner than expected. By the look in your eye I assume you have decided to join Rielle and aid her." Though caught off guard, and a little dumfounded, Vesth managed to keep a neutral face.

"I have considered it." He said, noncommittally. Rielle/Solidus nodded. "Good. If we are to succeed in gathering quickly enough we must split up. Rielle will go to Hortaal to speak with the High King, then to the moon witch forest to find one who would join our task." Vesth sat thoughtfully for a moment.

"Is splitting up a wise decision?" He asked. Rielle/Solidus shrugged.

"Probably not, but we have little choice. You must go to Laytrow, to a settlement to the north of the capital. There you will find a knight, his pennant will display a diving hawk. You must enlist him to our cause any way you can. When you have him, take him to the cabin at the highest peak in the Mercury Mountains. The path there is cleansed of evil and there is food and shelter. We will meet you there in two weeks time." Vesth nodded reluctantly.

"Very well. I will do as you ask." Rielle/Solidus nodded.

"Good, make haste, we have little time to spare." Blue color returned to Rielle's eyes.

"There is a split in the road just up ahead. If you take it, you will be at the Great Southwestern Gate in a little less than two days. After that any number of roads will suffice." Rielle told him, Solidus's voice disappearing. Vesth nodded quietly, then turned and kicked his mount into a run.

When they reached the turn in the road they stopped and Rielle gave Vesth any extra food she had in her pack. "Travel quickly and you should get where you're going in a week, maybe a day or two more." Rielle told Vesth. Vesth nodded.

"Be careful when you go to the Moon Witch Forest. There are a great many stories about that place." Rielle nodded.

"I will be fine. Worry about your own task and meeting us at Solidus's cabin in the Mercury Mountains." Vesth saluted and bowed, then leapt into his saddle and headed off down the road. Rielle watched him go, then turned her own horse and set off. Less than an hour of steady riding brought her within sight of the Capital city of Hortaal, Terramine.

The land for a mile around had been cleared so that everything could be seen from the watch towers that dotted the outer wall of the city. The city itself was made of solid stone, seemingly flawless in appearance, without visible seams.

"*High King Hortaal used his power to bind each stone together so that the city would seem to have grown from a mountain.*" Solidus told Rielle. Rielle nodded and answered aloud. "He wanted the city to appear as he wished his people to become, strong and immovable."

"*I am glad to see that you have learned your history.*" Solidus stated. Rielle nodded again.

"It can be very useful as an ambassador to be able to flaunt your history." Rielle nudged her horse to a faster pace and she soon rode through the main gate. She expertly navigated the streets and dropped from her saddle at the palace gates. The guards, after only a moment's pause, quickly stepped aside and called for the gates to be opened. Rielle stepped through importantly and handed her reigns to a stableman who was waiting on the other side.

"I wish to be conducted to see my dear cousin immediately." Rielle stated officially. Immediately orders were shouted and several guards formed around Rielle and marched off as she turned and headed for the castle gates. Once inside, the guards formed a column on either side of her and marched as her escort to the throne room. The doors to the throne room were pulled open as she approached and she stepped through, leaving her guards behind.

High King Morien Toriel sat on his throne, patiently waiting with a carefully concealed smile on his face. He was not a large man, but his muscles stood out on his arms, and his hand rested with an easy familiarity on the pommel of the sword at his side.

"Greetings to you, High King of Hortaal, Morien Toriel, king and kin." Rielle said grandly and bowed. The king's smile broadened.

"Rise, Ambassador Rielle. Welcome home cousin." Rielle straightened.

"There are a great many things which I would tell your highness, but I think it would be best that I speak them only to your ears. It is unthinkable that an enemy could have penetrated into your court, High King, but I have seen a great many things I wish to convey that I would not wish to accidentally find its way to the wrong ears." The High King's smile faded into a neutral line.

"I will grant the ambassador secret audience." He said. Immediately, a guard at the door clapped his hands twice and the few people who were in the throne room quietly left and the door was pulled shut behind them.

"What is it you wish to say, cousin?" The high king asked. Rielle told her story in the same way she had told it to the king in Gentry. The high king nodded and listened, but no emotion ever played across his face. Rielle finished with Solidus's warning to defend the cities during the Blood Moon Cycle.

"Yes, I heard from Commander Dalthis that we should be prepared for such." The high king nodded as he spoke and then sat silently, contemplating what had been said. Rielle stood quietly, waiting for him to speak again. Several moments passed before Rielle suddenly seemed to be able to feel something else in the room, watching them.

"*Close your eyes and steady your breathing.*" Solidus told her. She did as she was asked and only barely managed to avoid a sharp intake of breath as Solidus took control of her body. As soon as it was done, Rielle could feel a taint in the air.

"*It is the same as in the temple of Tyr Anon.*"

"*There is a demon here.*" Solidus replied. They waited in the silence for a few more seconds. Then, without warning, Solidus sprang into action. A man in dark, Telatian clothing dropped from the ceiling above the throne. In the same instant, Solidus drew his sword and sent it flying through the air. The high king, noticing the motion, leapt from his throne, drawing his sword as he rolled to his feet. Solidus's sword met the Telatian as he fell, and the force of the blow pierced his left shoulder and pinned him to the wall behind the throne. The high king looked at the groaning man on the wall, then to Rielle. He immediately noticed her eyes had changed color.

"The stories say that the great mage Solidus was so skilled in the magic of balance that his eyes turned silver and one could see all the balance and power of the world flowing through them." Rielle/Solidus glanced at the high king.

"It is good to see that my teachings to Hortaal Lyvinius have not been entirely lost. I would discuss it, but right now there are more important things to hold our attention." The high king turned back to the Telatian.

"So the Telatians have begun to send assassins to try and weaken us." Rielle/Solidus nodded.

"*Rielle, I will return control of your body to you. You will need to draw the demon from this man. I will walk you through it.*" Before she could complain, Rielle felt herself drawn to the front of her mind.

"Your highness, please keep watch while I attempt to question this man." The high king simply nodded, seemingly unconcerned that Rielle's eyes and voice had returned to normal. Rielle stepped behind the throne and stood directly in front of the moaning Telatian.

"*Place your hands together, in front of you as if praying.*" Solidus told her, and she did as she was told. "*Good, now will your power to beat, then visualize this man's inner power.*" Rielle nodded and closed her eyes, the beat of her power already beginning to quicken. When it reached its peak, Rielle turned her attention on the man pinned to the wall. She could see the ebb and flow of his power as it pulsed through the channels of his body. When she found his source, Rielle shuddered and flinched away. His inner power was like an orb of light that beat like a heart and sent warm light throughout his body. But around that orb of light was what seemed like a dark flame, burning away at the edge of it. Each beat of the orb flooded light through the body, but it was tainted by the dark flame.

"Now that you can see it, imagine a glass vial that draws in the flames from the body. Imagine this vial forming between your hands, made of your own inner power and open your hands to make way for it." Rielle nodded and made sure she was standing tall. At first the image was difficult for Rielle to create, it kept slipping and changing, refusing to remain solid. After a few moments, she tried to imagine the vial as its own small shield and the image quickly hardened. Directing her inner power to her hands, Rielle pulled them apart and willed her power to fill the image of the vial.

"Well done." Solidus said. *"Now, imagine that the flames inside the man's body are drawn into the vial. It may take several moments to succeed in gathering it all. Once you have gathered all the flames into the vial, imagine a stopper closing it and barring the flames from leaving."* Rielle once more did as she was told. The vial seemed to tip towards the man and the flame began to draw into it. It was difficult for Rielle. She could not force the flame to be drawn from the man any more than a trickle at a time, no more than a thread. The flame fought back, trying to yank free from the vial it was being pulled towards, but Rielle would not let it go. Several minutes passed before Rielle had gathered the flames into the vial. She quickly imagined a stopper plugging the end and sealing the flames inside.

"Good." Solidus said. *"Very good, now open your eyes and stare straight ahead and tell the demon to show itself and speak with you."* Rielle opened her eyes and could see that the space between her hands was rippling as if the air were hot, the same way she had seen it happen when she watched Solidus draw the demon from the man at the Great Gate.

"I command the demon that possessed this man to show itself and speak to me." Rielle said, focusing her words on the space between her hands and trying to emulate what she had heard Solidus do at the Great Gate. The air was suddenly cold and the space between Rielle and the man pinned to the wall rippled and warped as a figure appeared. Rielle inspected the demon. It was thin, as if it were simply bone covered with skin, and it had long talons at the end of its three-fingered hands. It had short skeletal wings that somehow held it aloft and its entire body was a slick, oily black.

"Ask for its name, knowing a name gives you a small amount of power over the creature." "What is your name?" Rielle asked. The demon turned it's beady yellow eyes to her. "Why should I answer?" It hissed. Rielle scoffed.

"You are in no position to argue." She told it. "I have the power to either destroy you or send you back to the Chaos unharmed. How you choose to cooperate will determine what happens to you." The demon glared at Rielle for several moments before answering.

"I am Ordinaisilac." Rielle nodded carefully.

"And who was it who sent you here and what was your mission?" The demon's hatred was very much apparent.

"A black robed priest in a black stone city sent me. I was

to kill the High King after I discovered if the rumors of the death of the great Silver Mage were true." Rielle frowned.

"Well, as you can see, I am alone in my journey here. And if you heard my story to the high king you will also know that Silver Mage Solidus sacrificed himself to save my life."

"*Ask how long he has had a host.*" Solidus said.

"I have one more question before I decide what to do with you." Rielle told the demon. "How long have you had this man as a host?" The demon made an angry noise.

"Almost a full moon." Rielle nodded and then took on an expression as if she were making a difficult decision.

"*To send him into the Chaos, you must extend your inner power before you and imagine a tear opening between the elements. Do not let it grow too large or you risk other demons coming through. Once the tear is open, press your hands together and imagine the Vial breaking and sending the flames through the tear and the tear sealing behind it.*" Rielle took a few moments to make sense of her instructions and then extended her power to open the tear.

"I have decided to send you back into the Chaos, Ordinaisilac," She placed specific emphasis on the demon's name. "But know that, should I encounter you again, I will not do so a second time." Once she had managed to create the tear, Rielle pressed her hands together and crushed her image of the vial. The demon shattered into a thousand pin points of light that were pulled into the tear. The flame disappeared into the Chaos and Rielle set to trying to close the tear she had made.

For several seconds she almost lost control and let the tear widen, but eventually she managed to cause the elements to form a web over the tear and solidify. When she was finished,

Rielle willed the beating of her inner power to slow back to its normal pace. She immediately felt the strain and was forced to lean against the side of the throne. The High King sheathed his sword and quickly stepped to Rielle's side.

"Are you well cousin?" He asked. Rielle nodded slowly.

"Yes, your majesty, I am well. The strain of using magic, especially something as advanced as that, is very tiring." The High King nodded.

"Shall I call the guards and have them bring you a chair?" He asked, ready to turn and call for the guards. But Rielle shook her head.

"That will not be necessary your majesty. Solidus wishes to speak with you and his strength will be sufficient to support me until I recover." The High King nodded as Rielle's eyes turned silver and she stood up straight.

"It is good to see that the High King of Hortaal is not afraid of magic as the rest of his people have grown." The High King nodded.

"I have long been taught the old ways. Though magic was lost to us many generations ago, I still know it is not an evil strength. Though, as the lost people of Alenon have unfortunately shown us, a thing does not need to be evil to be used wrongly." Solidus nodded, a little sadly.

"Indeed, but that is of little consequence. I wished to speak to you of your sword and the way you use it." The king nodded.

"Of course, Master Solidus. My sword was forged in a temple of Earth and Fire in Laytrow. It was a gift from the monks there." Solidus nodded and smiled, as if he knew something no one else did.

"Very good. And the way you wield it?" The High King nodded and drew his sword and held it in a stance similar to the one Rielle had been taught by Vesth. Rielle noticed the rearing dragon at the base of the blade.

"I was taught many fighting arts when I was young. The art I perform now is the culmination of all those years of learning. I took what styles I was taught and combined them into a single art. It took me years of honing until I had perfected it."

"My cousin, High King of Hortaal, is considered one of the greatest swordsmen alive." Rielle informed Solidus. Solidus nodded.

"And you are also a practitioner of Iai. To draw a sword in motion takes a great deal of skill." The High King nodded and returned his sword to its scabbard.

"Since the days of High King Hortaal it has been mandatory of the High King to learn Iai before he takes the throne. It is quick, precise, and impossible to read. It is the perfect art for protecting the king in his throne room. But to practice it on the battlefield, against an enemy, it is far too risky to use." Solidus chuckled and turned, grasping the sword in the wall. He removed the sword and flicked the blood from it as the body of the Telatian assassin fell to the floor. A smooth movement returned his sword to its scabbard.

"If one can react with speed, and has good timing, it is an art that is indispensable to any swordsman." Solidus suddenly stopped. He looked to the ceiling and smelled the air.

"Another one to join us has revealed themselves." He said. The High King looked around his throne room as if another assassin might drop from the ceiling.

"Who has revealed themselves?" The High King asked.

Solidus closed his eyes and turned slowly, reaching out one hand as if feeling the touch of something unseen.

"One who will join Rielle in bringing the world back into balance." He said as he turned. After a few steps he paused, his arm outstretched, and opened his eyes.

"Someone in that direction." The High King looked where Solidus was pointing. "Southwest. There is nothing in that direction except the Moon Witch Forest." Solidus nodded.

"And Bitreel." The High King looked back to Rielle/Solidus.

"You cannot be serious. Those who inhabit Bitreel and the Moon Witch Forest would not aid the outside world even if their lives depended on it. The people of Hortaal have hunted them for far too long. I wish it were not so, but even if I made a law that forbade anyone from harming those in the forest, there would be none who listened. The enmity between Hortaal and Bitreel has existed since the Purge. Only the line of High Kings of Hortaal that have been taught in the old ways have kept it from escalating to full blown war. If the army were not disciplined so rigidly to follow my commands, Bitreel would have been wiped out long ago. No one there will help anyone out here." Solidus half smiled.

"That may be so, but remember, I am not of this outside world. Rielle is of Hortaal, but she is now a mage and, as such, is now feared and hated by most of the known world. Of all people in this world, we are the ones who they may be convinced to follow. And it is only one of them that we need to convince. There is only one who can help restore the balance." The High King sighed.

"There is no point in arguing then. I could no more ask

you not to go than I could command High King Hortaal to rise from the grave. And I know better than to try and give my dear cousin Rielle an order she does not want to follow." Solidus chuckled.

"Indeed. But your worry is unnecessary. No harm will come of this journey." The High King nodded.

"Very well. If you cannot be dissuaded, then travel due southwest from here. The trees... change when you reach the Moon Witch Forest. Not far from there is a small village. If you pass too close to it, the guards there will stop you. Tell them the High King sends you in peace to speak with the Matriarch on a matter of great importance. They will conduct you safely to the Matriarch, who may be able to help you find the one you are looking for." Solidus nodded.

"Very well, Rielle will need supplies. I grow tired from controlling Rielle's body and must rest now, but I am sure she can take care of the details." The High King nodded once.

"Of course." Rielle's eyes returned to their natural color and she suddenly slouched. She took a few moments to compose herself and then spoke, Solidus's voice having disappeared.

"I will need several days rations and a good horse." She said. The High King nodded.

"Of course, but you must rest now. You are tired and in no condition to ride. You can set off in the morning when you wake. I will have everything prepared for you while you sleep." Rielle nodded and the High King called in a guard to escort Rielle to her quarters. Rielle was taken to a large set of rooms that were decorated lavishly with tapestries and paintings. A warm fire burned in the hearth set against the wall opposite the door. Two servant girls came into the room and quickly drew a warm bath in a copper tub and helped Rielle out of her travel clothes. She thanked them and dismissed them and settled into the bath to let the warmth soak into her tired body. She could feel Solidus in the back of her mind, as if he were pacing, but she was too tired to ask what he was thinking and simply lay quietly in the water.

Rielle jerked awake when the servant girls returned with fresh clothes and realized she had dozed off and the water was beginning to cool. The servants helped her out and dried her before helping her into her clothes. They bid her good night and, with her approving nod, they left Rielle to seek her bed.

Chapter Ten

Rielle woke to a quiet knock the next morning. She stood, finding she was much refreshed from the night before, and made her way to the door. When she opened it she found one of the servant girls from the previous night standing outside. The servant girl quickly bowed before speaking.

"High King Morien Toriel expressed his thoughts that you would wish to get an early start today." She said. "He wished to see you before you departed." Rielle nodded.

"You may tell my cousin that I will meet with him in the throne room before I depart." The servant girl bowed again and rushed away as Rielle shut the door again. Rielle quickly dressed, throwing Solidus's cloak around her shoulders and tying his sword to her waist. She looked at the bow and, after a few moments of thought, took it as well and slung it over her shoulder.

She quietly left her room and made her way to the throne room where she waited to be introduced before entering. The High King sat, speaking with one of his advisors when Rielle entered. Rielle noticed that the Telatian assassin had been removed and the wall and floor had been cleaned. Only a small crack in the wall showed where Solidus's sword had pinned the man. Rielle bowed.

"You requested my presence your majesty?" The High King smiled.

"You look much rested cousin. I hope you slept well." Rielle nodded politely.

"Yes your majesty, my accommodations were much appreciated." The High King nodded.

"Good. I have just been informed by my adviser that your horse and supplies are ready for your journey." The High King motioned to the man beside his throne. "You may leave when you are ready. Is there anything else you will need for your journey?" Rielle shook her head. "No, your majesty, what you have provided is enough. And I will be reuniting with my escort shortly." The High King nodded.

"If you will soon be with Captain Vesth of Gentry I am sure you will be safe. I have heard he is a fine officer." Rielle nodded.

"He is a very fine officer, and loyal. I will be safe in his care." The High King nodded once again.

"Very well, then I will no longer keep you from your task. Be sure to return again when you can cousin, it is a joy to see you." Rielle smiled.

"Of course, your majesty. I bid my cousin farewell." Rielle bowed and the High King nodded his head in return. Rielle straightened and exited the throne room. Outside, a guard was waiting for her and offered to show her to the stables. Rielle nodded and followed the man out into the courtyards and across them to the stables. There, a young boy waited with the reigns of a tall grey stallion held tightly in one hand. He looked nervously at the large animal as he held the reigns out to Rielle, who took them with a smile. The little boy scampered away and disappeared into the darkness of the stable.

"It would be wise not to let on exactly where we are going. Anyone here who sees you head out the south gate and then directly to the Moon Witch Forest is sure to remember it." Rielle nodded slightly.

"I agree. We should do our best to distract attention from our actual destination." This said, Rielle thanked the guard who had led her to the stable and then mounted her new horse. The stallion was steady and sure footed, waiting for a command from his rider. Rielle tapped his flanks lightly with her heel and he started off without hesitation. Rielle rode through the streets to the north gate, sitting proudly on her mount. The guards there let her through with a bow and she urged her horse into a trot. She rode easily over the flat ground towards the forest, waving and nodding to those working in the fields. She reached the forest and rode steadily for several hundred yards before pulling her stallion up short.

She looked around to make sure no one was following her or would see where she went, then quickly turned and headed west into the forest. The stallion pushed easily through the undergrowth as he picked his way around the trees. Rielle brushed branches aside in annoyance when they caught at her, but stubbornly continued to head west. Eventually she came across a game trail that headed south west and Rielle turned and followed it. It was not long before Solidus spoke.

"There is a magic you should learn." He told her.

"What help will it be?" Rielle asked. She could almost feel Solidus shaking his head. *"You should not think to learn only those things which may be useful to you. Learn all you can, at some point in your life you will find a reason to use that knowledge. But, to answer your question, what I am going to teach you is a nearly fundamental magic."* Rielle nodded.

"Of course, I apologize, I will keep an open mind. What is it that I must learn?"

"I'm going to teach you how to create light." Rielle almost felt a little discontent with the thought of something so seemingly simple. She could feel Solidus's amusement. *"Light is an invaluable and versatile skill to learn. There are always times when you find yourself in a dark place in need of light. Light can show your way, or blind an enemy. It can shed light on things that are hidden, or hide them from sight. It can provide a soft glow, intense heat, or form a simple distraction. If you learn to create light, you can find an infinite number of ways to use it."* Rielle was surprised by how Solidus had turned the simple idea of creating light into a complex skill with multiple ways to apply it.

"I am prepared to learn." She replied.

* * *

Rielle sat beside a small fire, concentrating on a point just above her open palm. The air there rippled and bent, like a long empty road on a hot summer day beneath the sun. A glow, so faint that it was barely discernable, tried to build in that ripple. After several moments of struggle, the glow faded away and Rielle dropped her hand tiredly to her side.

"Why is it so difficult? It sounds simple." She said to no one. Solidus answered from inside her mind.

"The sun shines brightly in the sky. The idea is simple, but can you explain why the sun shines? Why it rises and sets each day? The reason you can feel it's warmth on your skin? Just because an idea is simple does not mean it is easy to understand and explain. Your light does not shine for you because you think of it as a meaningless thing that does not exist until you tell it to. But there is light inside of you at all times. Your life is fed by fire, and fire gives light. All you need to do is find that light, created by your very life, and will it to shine before you. It is life itself, not a tool to be used." Rielle nodded sullenly. Solidus chuckled lightly.

"Do not be discouraged, you have made good progress. You have learned to create the space where the light can manifest itself. You only need to learn to call it out. It cannot be forced, it just has to happen naturally." Rielle sighed.

"I have been trying for two days." She complained. "And it still won't come to me. I can't seem to get it right no matter what I do or try." Solidus chuckled again.

"Give it time." Rielle shook her head. She felt a little silly for arguing out loud with no one around.

"It feels strange to be arguing with a three thousand year old immortal being inside my head." She felt Solidus shrug.

"Three thousand eight hundred, and I am not immortal, only ageless." Rielle scrunched her eyebrows together.

"What is the difference?"

"Immortality means you cannot die. Agelessness, or Eternal Youth, simply means one does not age. It does not mean that one cannot die or be killed. Demons, Dragons, and the last Alenon Mages, are all ageless. The six Deities that created the world are Immortals." Rielle nodded slowly, not entirely sure that she understood.

"You need rest." Solidus told her. *"Sleep and we will continue onward in the morning."* Rielle yawned then nodded again before laying down on her bedroll. She fell asleep quickly and dreamed. When she woke, she could not remember the dreams, but she felt as if they had been important. Looking around she found that the fire had gone out and the sky was beginning to get light. She packed her camp and made sure her horse was watered at a nearby creek before starting off.

Half the day went by quietly. Sometimes Rielle would try to create the ball of light as Solidus had told her, but could never get it to completely form. Solidus would give her pointers and, sometimes, remain mercifully silent. It was about the time that Rielle was stopping for lunch that she began to feel it. A taint in the air, not unlike the feel in the temple of Tyr' Anon.

"What is that?" She asked aloud, as she took a piece of dried meat and began to chew. No answer was forthcoming. Rielle's chewing slowed and she swallowed her food.

"Solidus?" The taint in the air around her grew stronger. Rielle stood nervously, looking into the trees for a source. "Where are you Solidus?" She almost cried. Leaves rustled behind her and a stick snapped. The world seemed to slow down as Rielle began to turn. Out of the corner of her eye, she saw a figure leaping from the underbrush. Long black claws tipped its fingers, and sharp, pointed teeth set in a snarl decorated it's almost human face. The creature shrieked as it pounced, sickly thin muscles tightening and twisting under ash grey skin as it attacked. Suddenly, Rielle felt herself pulled to the back of her mind and felt herself grasp the sword at her side. The sword left it's scabbard, as if it had a will of its own, and struck the creature out of the air. It landed in a heap, it's shriek cut off, and lay still. The sword returned to its scabbard. The whole thing had happened so quickly that Rielle's eyes had barely had a chance to turn silver before they were changing back again.

"What was that thing?" She gasped as control of her body returned.

"*They are called Nibilus, and if they are here then surely Basilisk are as well.*" Rielle looked around frantically.

"Are there more?"

"*Yes.*" Solidus replied. "*But not yet near. They are looking for you, but you can feel the taint when they grow close. You must hurry. Ride due south, the Moon Witch Forest is near. I will explain later.*" Rielle leapt into her saddle and kicked her horse into a gallop. Branches stung her face as she raced through the trees. She bent low over her horse's back and tried to turn her face away from the oncoming tree branches. Then, all at once, the branches ceased to strike at her. She carefully turned her face upward and gasped at what she saw.

The trees had suddenly changed into monolithic giants, their branches extending out hundreds of feet above, blocking out the light of the sun. Rielle's horse raced easily between the gargantuan trees, each easily fifty feet across. Rielle sat in wonder for several moments before Solidus spoke to her again.

"*Turn west and ride hard, they have picked up your scent.*" Rielle kicked at her horse again and laid low. It was for this reason that she almost trampled two men that stepped from behind two trees several hundred feet away. Her horse skidded to a stop and reared, Rielle clinging to the reigns for dear life. She leapt from the stallion once he had calmed down and stood steady, she could already feel the taint beginning to grow around them.

"State you business in the Moon Witch..."

"You fools!" Rielle shouted. The man she had interrupted looked dumbstruck. "Creatures of unspeakable evil are chasing me and now you will have them catch me, here, near your village."

"*Tell them to get into the trees.*" Solidus instructed. Rielle waved her arms angrily. "Climb you fools, climb for your lives!" Both men jumped at Rielle's angry tone and then started expertly up the trees, clinging to the rough bark as if it were simply a ladder. Rielle was amazed for a moment, but then Solidus was speaking again.

"*There are too many for you to fight and I cannot risk taking control again. These creatures are tied to the chaos and if they see you under my control the demons could possibly discover me. Your only chance is to play on their fear of light. It burns them when they get too near.*" Rielle looked at her hands and shook her head.

"But I can't, I'm not ready yet."

"*You must!*" Solidus commanded. Rielle jumped and then nodded as she began to build her power. The air around her seemed to thicken and a foul stench of decay filled her nostrils. The air above Rielle's hand began to ripple. Her concentration wavered for a moment as she heard growls and moans among the trees. Rielle looked around and shuddered at the thought of a thousand unseen eyes staring at her. She quickly focused on her hand.

"*The light is in you already, you only need to call it out.*" Solidus reminded Rielle. Rielle focused inside herself and searched for something she could interpret as light. Several moments passed, but for all her searching, Rielle could find nothing. The growls around her grew louder and the undergrowth rustled beneath heedlessly placed steps. Rielle could see shapes moving around, just at the edge of her vision. Her breaths came in quick gasps as she tried to see what lay in wait in the shadows beneath the trees. And then they began to appear. More sickly, grey skinned creatures began to creep out from around the trees and spars undergrowth.

Rielle's inner power beat desperately. Keeping one part of her mind on her open hand, she quickly built the image of her shield around her and filled it with power. The purple dome of energy that was her shield surrounded her and the creatures flinched back momentarily from its sudden appearance. Half a dozen creatures now surrounded Rielle, pacing slowly, working up the nerve to attack. One of the creatures turned and leapt at Rielle, crashed into her shield, and was thrown back with a yelp. Rielle focused on keeping her shield intact as she felt the pressure where the creature had struck, her mind racing, trying to find a way to escape. Another creature attacked and was thrown back. Several more attempts were made, each time the attack was thwarted by the shield, and with each attack it became more and more difficult to maintain it. Rielle was standing, tears welling up in her eyes, watching as the pack of creatures circled carefully. Then, as one, they all turned and attacked. Rielle watched as one who was lost and whispered,

"If I have light inside me, please let it save me." All the power she had built drained from her as it filled her hand and became a bright, golden sphere. The creatures shrieked in fear and pain as they tried to turn and run in mid air. They crashed into the shield and it collapsed, allowing more light through to the open. The few creatures who fell at Rielle's feet smoked and shriveled, quickly reducing to dust. The creatures who were farther back began to burn and peel as they continued to shriek and scramble over themselves in an attempt to run. Rielle watched in relief as the creatures fled in terror, turning until she saw something that was not running.

At the edge of the light cast by the sphere, Rielle could make out the silhouette of a giant creature. It seemed built the same as the smaller creatures that had just fled, but it was well over twelve feet tall with a thick mane of hair on its back and skin that was almost black that made it difficult to distinguish from the shadows around it.

"*A Basilisk.*" Solidus warned. Rielle felt power flow from Solidus into her and the sphere in her hand grew brighter and flecks and veins of silver pierced through the golden light. A pained snarl issued from the silhouette before it turned and loped into the trees. Rielle could feel the taint lessening, and then, disappearing altogether. She closed her hand over the ball of light and extinguished it, the drained feeling that came with using magic settled over her and she slumped tiredly.

"*Well done, I will explain what those creatures are when our task here is done.*" Rielle nodded carefully before looking up into the trees.

"The danger has passed, you may come down safely now." She called. It took several minutes before the two men climbed back down to join Rielle, each looking around carefully to see that there were no more creatures waiting to attack. When they had reached the ground, Rielle bowed.

"I am sorry to have yelled and called you fools. The situation was dire." The guard who had spoken when they first appeared nodded.

"We understand, had we known what it was that followed you, we would not have interfered." Rielle stood straight and nodded.

"It is well that you did stop me, I was in search of your village. I am sent by the High King of Hortaal in peace to speak with your Matriarch on a matter of great importance." The second guard eyed Rielle suspiciously.

"Why should we trust a child of Hortaal?" Rielle nodded sadly.

"I understand your suspicion and wish that the relations between our two peoples were not so strained. But I assure you that the High King, as well as myself, have nothing but good intentions toward your people. The High King wishes the bloodshed could be stopped but he fears that, if he were to order your safety, it would only serve to incite the people to break the command and cause further bloodshed. The matter of which I must speak to your Matriarch is not on behalf of Hortaal, but is for the safety of all people the world over, no matter their descent or disposition." The second guard still looked unsure, but did not speak. The first guard nodded and spoke.

"We have seen that you can use magic. No one of Hortaal would practice it and still hold enmity towards our people here. The art of magic was lost to us long ago, but we are hated because our ancestors once used that power. We will honor your request and take you to the Matriarch."

"Thank you. I am honored by your trust." Rielle said, and

bowed again before following the guards as they turned and led the way into the trees. They led her deep into the forest, twisting and turning seemingly without direction. Rielle could not have said which direction they were facing at any given moment. The enormous trees each looked identical to her and their thick canopies efficiently blocked all view of the sky. The guards leading her stopped in front of an especially large tree and waited. Rielle debated with herself about whether or not to ask what was happening but, before she could decide, she heard the quiet creak of rope above her head. She looked up, and was amazed to see a simple elevator being lowered down to them.

Once it touched the ground the two guards held it steady while Rielle boarded, then stepped on and tugged one of the four ropes attached to each corner. The elevator started up and Rielle held tightly to the edge. Once they reached half way up, Rielle could see the village. The entire community was living in the tops of the trees. Houses and walkways and stalls all lined the trees, rope bridges connecting each tree to the ones next to it. People walked along the paths and bridges, talking and laughing with one another, some shopping, some simply moving from one place to another. Rielle marveled at the simple happiness with which each person walked.

"It has been some time since I saw people who were untouched by war and destruction." Rielle said. One of the guards nodded and looked around.

"In the trees we are safe from those who wish us harm. For so long it has been the people of Hortaal, but now it seems there are other dangers for us to beware of." Rielle nodded her agreement and remained silent. Two guards were waiting for them when they reached the village. One of the guards stepped off the elevator and took one of the guards waiting for them aside. When they returned, the new guard looked at Rielle with a mixture of amazement, respect, and suspicion.

"We will lead you to the Matriarch's home." He said. Rielle thanked the guard who had brought her to that point and bid him farewell as he returned to the elevator and started back down. She turned and followed the two new guards across one of the rope bridges and down a path. The guards themselves were respectful enough, but Rielle immediately noticed that the villagers all stared at her with intense anger and hatred as they passed by. Rielle shuddered and kept her eyes on the back of the guard in front of her.

Eventually they came to a hut that was larger and more elaborately decorated than the others. One of the guards held a woven cloth door aside and bid Rielle to enter. When she was inside the guard spoke.

"Please sit and make yourself comfortable. The Matriarch will return soon to speak with you." Rielle thanked the guard and bowed. The guard bowed in return and then left. Rielle looked around the room carefully. There were herbs and roots hanging from the ceiling with no apparent order and a few glass vials of multicolored liquid sat on top of a small table with a mortar and pestle. More glass vials of similar liquids lined some shelves on one end of the room while shelves on the other were lined with scrolls of many shapes and descriptions. Rielle spotted a comfortable looking chair near the small table and sat down to wait. It was not long before an elderly woman, only marginally taller than Rielle, entered the room with an almost motherly smile.

"Would you like some tea dear?" The woman asked. Rielle nodded politely.

"Yes, thank you." The woman made her way to one of the shelves and took down a small clay pot. She sprinkled some of the contents into a small teapot and poured hot water into it from a larger teapot that had been sitting on a bed of heated stones. She waited a moment for the tea to steep, then poured the tea into two small cups and handed one to Rielle. Rielle excepted the tea with another thank you and sipped at it carefully. The hut was quiet for several minutes as they drank and the woman inspected Rielle. Finally, the woman broke the silence.

"It has been a great many years since we had a visitor come to our small village. Not one from Hortaal, and even longer since we had one that did not wish us harm." Rielle nodded.

"I am ashamed for my countrymen. My cousin, The High King, wishes nothing more than peace between our peoples. He would pass laws to protect your people, if he thought anyone would listen. Unfortunately, he fears that such an act would only drive the people of Hortaal to hunt you all the more." Rielle felt like she was repeating herself needlessly. The woman nodded. "Morien Toriel is still the High King is he not?" At Rielle's nod the woman continued. "He always did have a certain presence of mind that I admired. I also agree that a command to leave the people of Bitreel alone would only escalate the violence." Rielle nodded again and took another sip at her tea.

"The people of Hortaal still fear magic and think that magic is practiced here, though your guards have told me that is not the case. I wish that my country would listen to reason." The woman nodded.

"It is true that magic was lost to us many generations ago. But you came to us, sought us out. Do you not also fear magic?" Rielle smiled and held her hand palm up as Solidus had taught her. She found that calling the light was much easier now that she had already managed it once. A softly glowing ball of golden light appeared above her hand and the woman's eyes widened. "What reason is there to fear magic? It is like a sword, an arrow, or an ax. A simple tool that gives no reason to fear it. Only the one that wields it can make it good or evil." She closed her hand around the sphere of light and it went out.

"*Well put.*" Solidus said simply. The woman blinked several times and sipped from her teacup.

"You seem to be a very bright young woman. What has brought you here?" Rielle sat her tea on the table as Solidus gave her silent instructions.

"I have been instructed to come here and seek out a child." The woman gave her a strange expression.

"A child? What child would bring you here?" Rielle rubbed her hands together and picked her words carefully.

"It is difficult to explain. There is a child here, about twelve years old, who is very skilled and physically sound." The old woman nodded slowly and set her tea aside.

"I may know such a child. Why are you trying to find them?" Rielle took a slow breath. "We are at war. The world is at war. Balance in the world is shifting and falling apart. If the shift is not soon restored to balance, the world could come to an end. The child I am instructed to find will be a key part in restoring that balance." Suspicion filled the woman's features.

"Who is it who instructed you to find this child?" Rielle was silent for several seconds before giving a single nod.

"My mentor, The one who taught me to use magic. He is the one who saved your ancestors and brought them here during the purge." Suspicion was replaced by shock and Rielle nodded again.

"This village, and others in the Moon Witch Forest that make up Bitreel, were formed by those who had knowledge of magic. Knowledge that placed them in danger during the purge. Those who were found and saved by the Silver Mage, Solidus." The woman's shock slowly disappeared and, after several moments, she spoke again.

"The Silver Mage is the only one outside of this forest who would know of our history. You could only have been sent by him. I will summon the child that you seek." Rielle held up a hand and looked at the doorway for a moment.

"It seems that will not be necessary. The child I seek is coming to us as we speak." The woman gave Rielle a strange look, but nodded and sat back in her seat. Moments later a guard entered the hut, a ragged looking girl, about twelve years old, in tow.

"Matriarch, I caught Tiasia trying to sneak into the store rooms... again." The woman scowled at the little girl.

"How many times have you been told to stay out of there Tiasia? You know that the others will punish you severely if you are caught stealing their stores of food." The little girl shrugged and, unsuccessfully, tried to pull away from the guard.

"I was hungry." The Matriarch sighed heavily.

"You know better Tiasia, you should have just come and asked for food." Rielle half smiled.

"Let me have a closer look at you child." She said sweetly. Everyone looked at Rielle, who simply smiled and nodded. The Matriarch nodded to the guard.

"You may go, leave her here with me." The guard nodded then dropped the girl's arm, a little less than gently, and left the hut. Rielle motioned to the girl.

"Come closer. Tiasia, that was your name was it not?" The girl nodded and went to stand just in front of where Rielle was sitting. She had short black hair that was mussed and dirty with leaves and sticks. She had brown eyes and, though she had dirt smudged on her face, freckles could be seen dotting her cheeks and nose. She wore a dappled brown cloak, a tattered little tunic, and a pair of simple breeches. Rielle looked over her for several moments.

"She is the one." Rielle stated matter-of-factly. The Matriarch studied Rielle's face.

"Are you sure?" Rielle nodded.

"Quite. It is this little one that will be part of the balance. If it is alright with you, Matriarch, I would have this child leave and journey with me." The girl's face was suddenly the picture of excitement. The Matriarch looked back and forth between Rielle and Tiasia, struggling inwardly with the decision.

"You will take care of her?" Rielle nodded again.

"Of course. No harm will come to her if I can prevent it." The Matriarch looked back at Tiasia for several seconds before turning her head away and nodding.

"She may leave, with my blessing." Tiasia let out an excited squeak before she could contain herself. Rielle smiled.

"Go and gather your things." She glanced at the Matriarch before adding, "And do not stray between here and there or you may be left behind." Tiasia nodded vigorously and rushed from the hut. Rielle looked after the excited girl and then turned back to the Matriarch.

"There are other things of which you need to know. There are creatures in the forest, stalking all who they come across. They fear, and are hurt by, light. It would be best to keep the forest near your villages lit at all times to keep them at bay." The Matriarch nodded and motioned for Rielle to continue. Rielle looked around carefully to make sure that no one would hear her speak.

"There will soon be a Blood Moon Cycle." The Matriarch shuddered in her chair and only managed to speak in what was barely more than a whisper.

"When?"

Chapter Eleven

Vesth sat quietly on his horse as a knight in steel plate armor rode out of the castle, a pennant of a hawk diving past a sliver of moon on a field of blue at the tip of his lance. The knight came within fifty paces of Vesth and stopped.

"Your pennant displays a diving hawk." Vesth stated. "What is your name sir knight?" The knight removed his helmet, revealing blonde hair and green eyes, and placed it on the pommel of his saddle.

"I think that question applies more towards you good sir. It was you who called me out from my manor. State your intentions." Vesth watched the knight carefully, but gave a slight nod. "I am Captain Vesth Dagda, Captain of the armies of Gentry under the authority of Commander Thereon." Vesth stated formally.

"I was sent to find a knight whose pennant displays a diving hawk. I assume you are the only knight in Laytrow who has such." The knight nodded.

"I am. Why do you seek me?" Vesth sat still on his mount.

"I have answered your question with my name, sir knight, now I would have yours." The knight stared for a few seconds before answering.

"I am Sir Segine Memoria." Vesth half bowed in his saddle in acknowledgment.

"Sir Segine, I have come under orders to seek you out and escort you to a place to await further orders. This concerns the war with Telatia and, as I have been told, is of the utmost importance." The knight nodded, his features set in an indifferent expression.

"I understand your orders, and that you are honor bound to follow them through. However, your kingdom's orders do not hold sway over me. I cannot leave my manor. I must be here in case of a Telatian attack." Vesth could feel himself growing impatient with the knight, but carefully checked himself.

"I can understand your desire to protect the people of your manor, but the Great Gates have been destroyed. There will be no Telatian attack." The knights expression fell for a moment before he could take control of himself and return to his indifferent expression.

"How is this thing possible?" He asked. Vesth took a long slow breath before answering. "Magic." The knight quickly made the sign to ward off evil. Vesth nodded.

"The Hermit Mage came down from the Mercury Mountains to aid us in the war. I myself have been taught from birth that magic is evil, and I adhere to those teachings rigidly, but I did not feel evil in the Hermit Mage's presence. It was not Gentry that gave me the order to find you, It was the Hermit Mage. As much as I have despised magic, I would not disobey his orders, no matter the cost. His very existence demands respect." The knight sat quietly for several seconds before speaking.

"You think that I will follow an order given by a practitioner of magic? Even after I refused an order from Gentry?" Vesth shook his head.

"I expect no such thing, But I will follow my orders. You can come willingly, or I can take you by force, which I would not prefer. But, again, I will follow my orders." For a moment, the knight's expression turned to one of surprise and shock before returning to his indifferent mask.

"I admire your desire to follow your orders, as well as your tenacity to do what you think is necessary, but I will not be so easy to bully into following you." Vesth nodded. "Understandable, But this task truly is in your best interests. We work to stop Telatia, who has also began practicing magic, before they can do something unspeakable." The knight sat silently and Vesth continued.

"We have no way to combat magic on such a large scale. Despite its evils, we must ask one skilled in magic to aid us. I have spent a good deal of time in the presence of the Hermit Mage. He is not only a powerful magic user, but his skill with a blade is unsurpassed. Even I was no match for him, though I am considered to have no small amount of skill." The knight eyed Vesth, then he placed his lance in a slot against his saddle and tied it into place before dismounting.

"Dismount and let us duel. I would see your skill before I make my decision." Vesth nodded and slid from his saddle, easily landing on his feet beside his mount. The knight made his way to a point between their horses and drew his two-handed sword. Vesth immediately noticed the crouching dragon etched into the blade. Vesth half smiled to himself as he made his way out to meet the knight. He drew his own sword, being careful to keep the etching of the rearing dragon on his own blade turned away so the knight could not see it. Vesth stepped into position across from the knight and held his sword at the ready.

"I will attempt not to cause you any serious injuries, Captain." The big knight stated. Vesth nodded in return.

"I will also pull my blows if I can." The knight nodded and then leapt at Vesth with a dexterity that defied his large sword and heavy armor. Vesth quickly side stepped and struck at the knight's unprotected back. The knight reversed his blow in mid-air and managed to intercept Vesth's attack. Vesth deflected another blow, then tried to drop under the knight's guard. But as he rose back up, the knight released his sword, wielding it one-handed, and struck directly at Vesth with his empty hand. Vesth raised his sword and blocked the punch, sliding backwards on the dusty road from the force of the blow. It was then that the knight noticed the dragon on Vesth's blade.

"You are a master of the Rearing Dragon?" Vesth stood straight, his sword resting comfortably in his hand, but ready to spring into action should the need arise.

"I am." The knight eyed Vesth carefully.

"You told me that you were no match for the Hermit Mage, and yet you wield a Rearing Dragon blade. How is that so?" Vesth breathed slowly and let his heart rate return to normal. "Grandmaster Solidus, the Hermit Mage, Is a master of the Flying Dragon." The knight stared.

"There has been no recorded Master of the Flying Dragon since the teacher of High King Hortaal. Even High King Morien Toriel in Hortaal is not yet a Flying Dragon." Vesth nodded. "High King Morien Toriel is indeed one of the greatest swordsmen in a thousand years, but the Hermit Mage is far older than that. He is the very man who trained and taught High King Hortaal."

"Impossible." The knight said emphatically. Vesth simply shrugged.

"I am not one to say what is possible and what is impossible, I am only a soldier. But everything I told you is what I believe to be the truth. Master Solidus is far more skilled in mind and sword than I could ever hope to be." The knight studied Vesth for several moments before taking his sword in both hands again.

"Win our duel, and I will consider you truthful." Vesth stood still for a few seconds before nodding and returning his sword to its scabbard.

"Very well, you may begin. My sword will leave it's scabbard when it becomes necessary." The knight raised one eyebrow ever so slightly, but nodded. Vesth stood still, watching the knight as he circled, tensely waiting for the perfect moment to strike. When the knight did strike again, it was hard and fast. Each sword stroke caused the air to sing as Vesth sidestepped each attack.

Vesth's sword flashed when it finally left it's scabbard. The blade cut through the air and intercepted the knight's sword in mid-strike. The knight looked mildly surprised and pulled back to ready himself for another attack. Vesth quickly stepped forward in pursuit, keeping his sword pressed tightly against the knight's. The knight rapidly retreated, trying to free his sword from Vesth's advance. Then, in a move of desperation, the knight leveled another punch at Vesth, his other hand holding tightly to the two-handed sword.

Vesth stepped into the attack, avoiding the punch, and brought the pommel of his sword down on the knight's sword hand. The blow knocked the sword to the ground and, as it fell, Vesth reversed his sword and pressed it up against the knight's throat. Everything was still. Then Vesth removed his sword and placed it back in its scabbard, the knight took his sword and did the same, messaging his throat with one hand.

"I admit defeat. I consider what you have told me to be truthful." Clapping issued from one side of the road where they stood. Both men twisted and their swords were instantly in their hands.

"I do not think that will be necessary, Vesth." Solidus said with a grin. Vesth quickly returned his sword to its scabbard. Solidus stood before them, transparent and surrounded by a soft glow.

"Master Solidus, how is it you are here?" Vesth asked. Solidus's hands dropped to his side.

"It is a very complex magic that I do not think you really wish me to go into details about." Vesth quickly nodded.

"Of course. Where is miss Rielle? Is she well?" Solidus nodded with a chuckle.

"Yes, she is resting. She encountered some rather nasty creatures, with which she dealt admirably. Her new companion is also with her." Vesth blinked and Solidus nodded again.

"Yes, you will meet her when you escort Sir Segine to my home on the peak." Sir Segine lowered his sword carefully.

"How do you know me sir? I do not think we have met." Vesth looked at the big knight. "This, Sir Segine, is Grandmaster Solidus." Sir Segine looked back and forth between Vesth and Solidus.

"Your Master Solidus is a ghost?" Vesth couldn't answer and Solidus laughed.

"No Sir Segine, I am not a ghost. This is simply an image of myself. At present I do not have a body and I live inside the mind of Rielle, who you will meet when you arrive in the Mercury Mountains. But that is not important for the moment." Solidus's face sobered.

"You must spend the night here, then travel as swiftly as you can and do not travel at night. The Telatians are releasing creatures that have been sealed away for uncounted centuries. These creatures are very dangerous and are controlled by much larger creatures that are similar to the smaller ones, but they cannot be touched by light as it burns them severely. Stay in the manors of other knights or in towns as you travel until you reach my home. Make haste, our time grows short." Vesth nodded.

"As you say, Master Solidus." Solidus nodded in return and then faded away. Vesth sighed heavily.

"The longer I journey on this quest, the more unpleasantly surprised I become." Sir Segine returned his sword to the scabbard at his side and moved to his horse.

"Evening draws near and night comes quickly. You are free to stay in my manor as your Master Solidus has suggested. We will set off at first light." Vesth nodded and took the reins of his horse in hand.

"I follow your lead Sir Segine."

* * *

Vesth sat in Sir Segine's large dining hall eating the large breakfast that had been placed before him. Sir Segine sat at the head of the table sharpening the nicks out of his blade with a whetstone.

"We may begin our journey to the Mercury Mountains when you have finished your meal Captain Vesth." The knight was saying. Vesth nodded and swallowed the food in his mouth. "That is good. However, you do not need to continue calling me captain. I am a captain of the Gentry army and navy, but on this quest I hold no such authority. I am simply, Vesth." The knight glanced at Vesth out of the corner his eye as he rubbed at a particularly stubborn notch in the blade.

"A man is nothing but what his name says about him. You are captain. It shows your skill and determination as well as your loyalty. Why would you give that up? Why give up your name so that others may not know you for what you are?" Vesth let out a short laugh.

"I understand that, to a knight, his name and honor mean everything. But for a soldier of Gentry, all honor is for our kingdom, we keep none for ourselves. My title is to let those soldiers of lower rank know that through hardship I have fought for Gentry and brought it honor, earning the honor of being able to give orders to others to bring further honor to our homeland. But what I do now is not to bring honor to Gentry. I am not here to give orders to others. Here, everyone is equal. Everyone does their part as it should be, not for honor, but for the good of all peoples in all kingdoms." Vesth looked back to his plate, with sudden understanding.

"Everything in balance." Segine said, placing his whetstone

in a pouch at his side and returning his sword to its scabbard. Vesth nodded. The knight stood.

"If you are ready, our horses are packed with rations enough to make the journey. If we travel quickly we can reach the manor house of Sir Dreagnor Nilancint before nightfall." Vesth stood.

"Then we should make haste. I did not like the sound of Master Solidus's warning yesterday. I think it wise to follow his instruction." The knight nodded and swept out of the hall as servants came in to clean up what was left of the meal. The two men rode out of the gate, Segine pausing only long enough to give a few instructions to the guard there before they started down the road. They rode for most of the day, talking very little. At one point Vesth asked how long it would take to get to the Mercury Mountains. Segine thought carefully before answering. "By the end of today we will reach the manor of Sir Dreagnor. From there it is almost two full days to the town of Meria, perhaps three if we stopped in Yal' Tora." Vesth shook his head.

"We cannot risk the time." The knight nodded in return.

"From Meria it is a full day's ride to the base of the Mercury Mountain." Vesth shuddered.

"I do not like the thought of entering those mountains. No one venturing into them has ever come back out. Miss Rielle once told me that it is because Evil was sealed in the mountains to maintain balance when Alenon was destroyed." Segine glanced across at Vesth.

"Did you not also say that Ambassador Rielle entered those same mountains and left them again, with the Hermit Mage in tow?" Vesth nodded.

"Yes. Master Solidus says that he cleansed the path that lead to the peak. He says it is safe to travel as long as you stay on the path." The big knight nodded.

"Then I, for one, have no qualms about entering the mountains. If there is a safe path with no danger, I see no reason to fear. And if there are creatures there that would attack us, I feel confident that they are no match for ones such as us." Vesth shrugged.

"You are surely correct, Sir Segine, but I will remain skeptical until I have seen for myself. I would rather be worried and fearful for little reason than travel a dangerous path without caution." Segine nodded again.

"A strategic process of thought that I will agree upon. However, when we are not traveling amongst the civilized world, you have no need to call me by title. You forsake your title for the sake of the people and you are correct. Outside of Laytrow I am simply Segine Memoria, no longer a knight of stature." Vesth half smiled and then nodded.

"Welcome to you, Segine Memoria, We are glad to have you with us on this journey." The knight banged his fist against his chest.

"And I am proud to join you." They continued the rest of the day in silence, all the while Vesth thinking that the knight would be proud doing almost anything. They reached the manor of Sir Dreagnor just as the sun was beginning to set. Sir Dreagnor was an older man with graying hair and a heavily lined face. He was covered in scars collected from years of tournaments and duels, fighting for the honor of knighthood. The old knight agreed to let them spend the night and brought them inside to a hot meal. They slept well and woke in the morning with knights walking the halls and grounds. Vesth watched warily as a group of guards rushed past him and Segine as they went out to meet Sir Dreagnor.

"What is all the fuss this morning, Good Sir Dreagnor?" Segine asked as they drew near. The old knight turned to them, weariness in his eyes.

"Good morning, Sir Segine, I trust you slept well and that your breakfast was suitable." Sir Segine nodded.

"It was all very satisfactory, thank you. What has your men so tense this morning?" The old knight looked around the grounds as knights and guards scrambled from one place to another. "Last night there was an attack outside the manor walls. Nobody saw what it was, but it killed a guard and wounded another before it ran off. I brought everyone inside and locked the gates."

"I think that was very wise." Vesth stated. The old knight turned to Vesth.

"Do you know what it is that has attacked my guards?" Vesth licked his lips and scratched at his chin as he carefully thought through his words.

"I have heard intel from outside sources that said the Telatians found a certain type of creature that had been sealed away in the mountains centuries ago. We have no name for it, but it is said that they are strong and fast and are controlled by the Telatians through much larger creatures that are similar to the smaller ones. All we know for sure is that they are severely burned by light and fear it. I would suggest that you keep your people indoors at night and keep watch fires burning at all times." The old knight nodded.

"I agree, that is a sound course of action. Even if they are not burned by light, the fires will at least allow us to see their approach. Will you be leaving immediately?" Vesth nodded and Segine spoke.

"We are to meet with someone who will be giving us further orders in Meria." The old knight looked to Segine.

"Will you be stopping in Yal' Tora?" Segine shook his head. "I am afraid not. We must arrive in Meria as soon as possible. We will travel until nightfall and then stay with one of the farmers along the main road there." The old knight nodded again.

"Very well, safe journey to you." Both Vesth and Segine half bowed and then quickly mounted and left the manor, heading south. This time no words passed between them. Both men sat upright and alert, looking for any signs of danger.

The capital city, Yal' Tora, drifted by them, a few miles to the east as they rode. They entered cultivated land that was divided into large fields. Some grew wheat, some corn, and others held livestock or horses. As the sun set they found a farmer that was willing to let them spend the night and locked their horses in the barn. After dinner with the farmer and his wife they took turns standing guard at a small window by the door. When the farmer asked what they were looking for Vesth simply replied that there had been reports of dangerous creatures around. "Perhaps wolves." Segine suggested. "The reports aren't clear. But we would rather be safe than sorry." The farmer shrugged and left it at that. The night was uneventful but both Segine and Vesth noticed soft growling sounds and the occasional movements outside when it was their turn to stand guard. In the morning they thanked the farmer for his hospitality quickly saddled their horses and set off. Riding most of the day brought them to a low hill looking over the town of Meria.

They rode down into town and found an inn that was not too crowded and stabled their horses. Segine paid for their rooms and Vesth found a corner table in the common room and sat with his back against the wall. Segine soon joined and sat near Vesth, but turned enough to see the entire room.

"Our rooms are at the end of the hall on the second floor, directly across from one another." Vesth nodded.

"Good." They sat silently for several minutes, declining to order from the maid as she swept by. Vesth breathed deeply.

"Something does not feel right." He stated. Segine looked at him across the table.

"You sense it as well?" Vesth nodded.

"There is something off in this town. I don't know what it is, but I do not like it." The big knight nodded his agreement.

"It is definitely more tense here than last I visited. Maybe we should investigate." Vesth opened his mouth to speak, but was interrupted.

"That would not be wise, Vesth Dagda of Gentry." The voice was drawn out in a long hiss. A man in a dark cloak rose from a table a few paces away from them.

"I think you would be more wise to stay out of affairs that do not concern you." Vesth nodded and seemed unconcerned, though Segine could see that Vesth's hand was resting carefully on his sword.

"That may be true, but I think that, by revealing yourself, you have only served to make me more inclined towards investigating further." Vesth looked around the room. It was abandoned. The innkeeper, the maids, and those few people who had been there escaped into the kitchen when the cloaked man had spoken.

"You must be truly horrible to behold, seeing as all the other guests have fled." The man scoffed.

"They are smart enough to know when something does not concern them. You would have been wise to do the same." Vesth raised an eyebrow.

"Would have been? Is that a threat? Sir Segine, Is this man threatening us?" Segine rose from his chair, flexing his shoulders and placing one hand on the sword at his side.

"I do believe he is." Vesth nodded once.

"You speak often of wisdom, yet you do not practice it. You would have been wise not to start this confrontation, but now it seems that we have come to a disagreement." The man tilted his head to one side.

"So it seems, but do not be hasty. Perhaps we can resolve our differences without violence." Vesth shrugged indifferently.

"I do not think that is an option, but I am listening. What did you have in mind?" The man tilted his head the other way.

"Leave the city, go your separate ways. There is no need for you to reunite with the Hortaal ambassador. This quest you find yourself pursuing is not yours to bear. Leave it to the ambassador and return to your home. Promise this, and we may part ways in peace." Vesth almost laughed.

"Are you truly that desperate to stop us? Nothing will stop me from reuniting with Ambassador Rielle. I swore to protect her, and I will do just that." The man snarled under his cloak.

"If you will not choose to leave, then you will die." Segine drew his two-handed sword. "Just try it. Be prepared, however, for the consequences." The cloaked man growled and pulled a short sword from under his cloak, his hands were pale and clammy. Segine leapt at the man, swinging his sword as if to split him in two. The man in the cloak quickly stepped out of the knight's way and slashed at the knight with his blade. Segine turned and swatted the short sword aside and stabbed at the man's chest. The man dropped, Segine's sword catching the top of his hood and tearing the cloak from his shoulders.

Vesth quickly inspected the man. He was thin and pale with yellowed eyes and sharpened teeth. He was bald and his scalp was cracked and oozing a strange liquid. And a long tail covered in pale flesh extended from the base of the man's spine, a six inch black spike tipping it's end. The man dropped to all fours and struck at Segine like a scorpion. Segine quickly deflected the black tip with his sword. The man recoiled and struck again, this time avoiding Segine's sword and striking him in the left shoulder, piercing the knight's plate armor. Segine roared in pain and dropped his sword, taking hold of the man's tail. With a shout, Segine lifted the man by the tail and threw him across the room, the black spike tearing from Segine's shoulder.

The man landed with a crash, smashing one of the tables and several chairs. He rolled to his feet like a cat and turned on Segine again, charging at him with a shriek. Vesth left his chair at a run, leaping over the table and sprinting across the common room. The man struck at Vesth using his tail, and Vesth's sword left it's scabbard in a blur of motion. The creature shrieked again as Vesth deftly removed the tail and then twisted and planted his sword in the man's back. The man cried out and collapsed to the floor.

"Know this, demon host, we will fight you to the end. We will rejoin Ambassador Rielle and from there plan our assault of your masters. Try to get in our way again, and your end will not be so pleasant." Vesth removed his sword and decapitated the man where he lay and then wiped his sword off on the man's clothing before replacing it in its scabbard. Segine stumbled backwards and fell into a chair. Vesth turned and rushed to Segine's side, picking the large knight's sword off the floor.

"Where are you hurt?" Vesth asked. Segine's hand clutched at his left shoulder, clear liquid oozing from the wound beneath. Vesth slipped the knight's sword into its scabbard and then pulled Segine's hand out of the way and inspected the wound.

"It is a minor scratch." The knight insisted. Vesth shook his head as he prodded at the wound despite Segine's grunts of protest.

"This is deep, and it is already full of infection. You will not survive more than a couple of days unless something is done."

"I'm fine." Segine insisted again. "I've had much worse." Vesth scoffed.

"I have seen soldiers in the battlefield who died from wounds such as this. Once the infection has progressed this far, there is little that can be done." Segine frowned.

"Then what do you propose?" Vesth thought quietly for a moment.

"We should get to master Solidus as quickly as possible. He should be able to do something." Segine scowled.

"I will not be healed by magic." Vesth positioned himself under the knight's uninjured arm and helped him stand.

"You, my friend, have no choice." Vesth saw movement from the kitchen and glanced in that direction. The innkeeper, the cook, and one of the maids were standing just inside the door. "Innkeeper." Vesth called. "We will not be spending the night. However you may keep the payment. When I return from saddling our horses have a large sack with as many torches as you can find ready. We will need them tonight." The innkeeper stammered his understanding as Vesth helped Segine out the door and towards the stable.

They entered the stables and Vesth set Segine against one wall before going to saddle the horses. As he tightened the straps he glanced nervously out at the early evening sun. When the horses were saddled, Vesth helped Segine back onto his feet and up into his saddle. Once he was sure that the knight would not topple to the ground, he quickly made his way back into the inn. He returned moments later with a large sack of torches. He tied the sack to his own saddle and then mounted.

"Can you ride Segine?" Segine took hold of the reigns with his uninjured arm and nodded. Vesth nodded in return.

"Good, then we ride to the Mercury Mountains. We will ride through the night if we must." Segine nodded wearily in return.

13

Chapter Twelve

They left Meria and pushed their horses to a gallop the moment they left the gates. They flew across the plains, pushing the horses as fast as they could go, rarely slowing to a walk long enough for the horses to catch their breath before racing on again. By the time the sun was beginning to set, Vesth could see the forest and the Mercury Mountains in the distance. Vesth came to a stop to let the horses rest and had to catch Segine's arm to keep him from falling out of his saddle.

"Are you well?" He asked the knight. Segine tried to nod.

"Of course I am. I could travel another hundred leagues." The knight swayed in his saddle.

"I rather think not." Vesth said, leaping down from his saddle and pulling a length of cord from a pouch. "You couldn't stay in your saddle for five more minutes, let alone a hundred leagues." He forced the knight to lean forward then tied his arms around the horses neck.

"It will be uncomfortable, but you won't fall off this way." Vesth told him. Then he went to his saddle and removed a few torches from the sack and set them alight. He took one of the torches and stuffed it under Segine's belt, making sure it would not burn him.

"Whatever Master Solidus said was out here fears light. This should at least keep them at arm's length." Segine grunted but said nothing. Vesth turned to mount again and saw Segine's wounded shoulder. It was swollen and an angry red color, clear liquid continued to ooze from it. "It hasn't bled yet. You need to bleed to help fight the infection." Vesth said, sticking his newly lit torch upright in the ground. He quickly removed Segine's left shoulder guard. He inspected the wound for a few seconds then drew a short knife and inserted it into the injury. Segine groaned and tried to move. Vesth placed a hand on the knight's back and held him in place.

"I know it hurts friend, but you need all the time we can get." Vesth added pressure to the knife and then quickly withdrew it. Crimson blood flowed from the wound. Vesth made a few more cuts and then tore a scrap of cloth from his tunic and stuffed it into the wound, tying the shoulder guard back in place over the top. Vesth heard a growl not far away and looked over his shoulder. Behind them, just outside of the light cast by the torches, stood a sickly thin creature with ashen grey skin and long claws. It's face was oddly almost human, but when it growled again Vesth could see needle sharp teeth.

"So this is what Solidus spoke of." He muttered. He turned to face it and drew his sword, blade flashing in the torch light. The creature flinched back a couple of paces with a hiss. Another growl came from behind Vesth. Vesth looked around with one eye and saw another creature there. Vesth growled back.

"With the sun down these things are going to be after us by the dozens." He looked around, thinking carefully, as three more creatures surrounded them but staying outside the ring of torchlight. Then the torch that had been thrust into the ground caught Vesth's eye.

"Ok then." He said to no one in particular. He took hold of the reigns of both horses and wrapped them around his hand. "Since the sun has gone down, I will just have to make it as bright as day without it." He stood silently, breathing carefully for a few moments. Then he turned and kicked the torch towards one of the creatures. It shrieked and fled as Vesth leapt up into his saddle. The dry grass caught fire and in seconds it was a roaring inferno. The creatures scattered with shrieks of fear and pain. Vesth kicked his horse into a run and straight through the wall of flames.

"It seems I underestimated you." He told the horse on the other side. "It seems you were worth the price I paid for you after all." The horse looked at him rather calmly as if to ask why they were not still running. Vesth nodded. "You will have your chance to run, but we must stay near the fire. Now if the wind were to start blowing in the direction of the mountains it would drive the fire fast enough for you to..." Vesth stopped as the wind picked up and began to blow towards the Mercury Mountains.

"That's strange." Segine muttered in a pained voice. Vesth nodded.

"Indeed it is, but I will not begrudge such fortune." The fire had reacted immediately to the stiff wind and roared with angry life. It rushed over the dry plains so quickly that it was far ahead of them when Vesth had finally turned the horses and pushed them into a gallop. They raced after the wildfire, staying as close as they dared to avoid the creatures which Vesth could still hear growling and barking to one another over the roar of the fire.

They ran on for what seemed to be an eternity to Vesth until they suddenly came upon the forest. The first trees burst into flames and the flames which had been ten feet tall grew to over forty." Vesth reigned in the horses who danced nervously from side to side. He looked behind them and saw hundreds of sickened yellow eyes reflecting the firelight back at him.

"Don't look at them Vesth!" Vesth whipped his head back around to stare at the wall of fire. He had recognized Rielle's voice immediately. There was a few seconds of nothing, and then the flames directly in front of them were thrown aside as if by a powerful wind. Rielle stood amongst them, surrounded by a purple glow.

"Through the fire Vesth, quickly!" She shouted. Vesth kicked his mount again and they raced past the wall of fire. Rielle held out her hand and caught Vesth's, swinging up into the saddle behind him. She slumped tiredly against his back.

"Quickly, we must get up the mountain. Solidus cannot manifest right now. He says that he must save his strength to save Segine." Vesth glanced back over his shoulder and watched as the fire spread.

"What of the fire? We can't let the villages around here burn to the ground because of what I did." Rielle shook her head.

"The Deity of Evil has agreed to control the fire. It will not spread where it should not." Vesth felt a knot in the pit of his stomach and Rielle seemed to sense it.

"The Deity of Evil is part of the balance too. He will help us as long as it proves to help him as well. It will cause problems for him if the fire spreads into the mountains so he will stop the fire when we reach the path to the peak." Vesth nodded and leaned forward. The horses raced through the trees and burst out into a clearing beside a high wall of cliffs.

"Turn right and follow the cliffs until you come to the corpse of a felle wolf." Rielle called. Vesth pulled on the reigns and turned to follow Rielle's instructions. They raced along the cliff, splashing across a small stream created by a spring, and rushed out into a clearing. Vesth pulled up short when he saw the shadowy mass of fur that he assumed was the dead felle wolf. Rielle pointed at a narrow opening in the cliff.

"There. That is the path that leads to the cabin. It is clear of dangers. We need to hurry so Solidus can look into Segine's condition." Vesth nodded and steered the horses towards the opening. The moment they stepped through the opening in the cliff Vesth felt a sudden chill wash over him from the mountains and out into the forest.

"The Deity of Evil is extinguishing the fires, as promised." Rielle stated. Vesth shuddered and kept moving. The ride up to the peak was easy and no more of the monsters appeared behind them. When they reached the top Rielle slipped off of Vesth's horse and took the reins from him. "Tiasia." She called. "Come quickly and tie these horses next to mine." Vesth dismounted and then watched in surprise as a young girl, no more than twelve, ran out of the small hut and joined them.

Vesth quickly untied Segine and helped him down before the girl took the reins of the horses and led them off around the hut. Rielle got under one arm and Vesth the other and they half led half dragged Segine into the hut. When they were inside, Rielle's eyes turned silver and Solidus spoke.

"He is in very bad shape. Help me remove his armor." He told Vesth. Vesth nodded and they quickly untied the bulky plate armor and set it aside. The young girl returned and Rielle/Solidus pointed to the heap of armor.

"Please take that armor into the meditation room little one." The girl nodded.

"Yes sir, mister Solidus." She gathered what she could into her small arms and dragged the rest towards a door at the back of the hut. Rielle/Solidus removed the scrap of Vesth's tunic and prodded at the injury. Segine groaned. Rielle/Solidus shook her head, tracing the lines of Vesth's cuts.

"You did well to make the incisions Vesth, but this is already beyond my power to heal." Vesth felt himself become angry.

"You sent me halfway across the world to find this man only to let him die from a minor injury he received because he was with me?" Vesth tried to refrain from shouting. Rielle/Solidus shook her head carefully.

"I didn't say that. I said it was beyond my power to heal. We will have to take him to Agamemnon." Rielle/Solidus rolled the groaning knight over and helped him stand. Vesth quickly supported him.

"How are we going to get to the Temple Island of Alenon in time?" Rielle/Solidus muttered a reply.

"There are ways." Rielle's eyes returned to normal.

"There is a cave a short way back down the path we took to get here, we must take him there." Vesth nodded and they started for the door. "Tiasia, come quickly." Rielle called. Vesth felt Segine flinch when they heard the girl drop the armor and come running.

"What should I do?" She asked. Rielle shook her head.

"Nothing right now, Tiasia. Everything will be provided where we are going." The little girl nodded and simply followed a few paces behind. They shambled down the path until they came to the small cave Rielle had spoken of. They went inside and laid Segine down next to a cold fire pit. Rielle pointed at the small pit and whispered a word. A small fire leapt up around the wood and Vesth could immediately feel the heat.

"It seems your skills are increasing." Vesth commented. Rielle nodded as she knelt down next to Segine.

"I have had a few days to practice and learn here while we waited for you." She pulled a handkerchief from her pouch and wiped the sweat from Segine's face. Vesth felt a tug at his sleeve and looked down to see the small girl standing beside him. She held out her hand and spoke.

"I am Tiasia, nice to meet you." Vesth hesitated for a moment before taking the girl's small hand in a handshake.

"I am Vesth, I am glad to meet your acquaintance as well." Tiasia looked at Rielle. "Oooh, he is very proper isn't he?" Vesth gave the girl a strange look and Rielle laughed. "Yes he is, but you get used to it after a while." Tiasia shrugged and squatted down next to Rielle.

"And this is the knight mister Solidus said was coming? He doesn't look very good." Rielle nodded.

"For some reason the infection is spreading very quickly through the rest of his body. It is going to be difficult to remove."

"Then what are we waiting for?" Vesth asked. Rielle looked out of the cave mouth at the mountains to the south east.

"The moon must rise before we can proceed. We are fortunate, tonight is a Bright Moon Cycle." Tiasia followed Rielle's gaze and then looked back to Rielle.

"What is a Bright Moon Cycle?" Rielle laughed patiently.

"It is a fancy name for the full moon." Tiasia made an O with her mouth and nodded. Vesth also looked outside.

"Why is it important that it is a full moon tonight?" Rielle pointed as the moon began to rise.

"You will see." The bright silver moon rose over the mountains, lighting up every detail almost like day. The light flooded into the cave and a grinding noise sounded from the back wall. They all turned to watch as a section of the wall slid down into the floor and revealed a large room on the other side. Rielle's eyes turned silver again.

"Help Segine to his feet, I must open the portal that will take us to Alenon." Vesth nodded and lifted Segine with a grunt. Tiasia, at a loss for any way she could help, simply followed behind Vesth, hoping he would drop something she could pick up and pretend it was very important that she carry it around.

They moved into the room and Vesth looked around quickly. The room was a large dome with nothing to adorn it's walls or floors save a set of rings standing upright on a raised dais on the opposite end of the room. The rings were of varying size, ranging from six feet across at the outer edge, to two feet across at the center. Each ring was an inch wide and had six clear, perfectly round, gems imbedded at equal intervals around them. At the center of all the rings was a single, large gem the same as those in the rings, but much larger.

"What is this place?" Vesth asked. Rielle/Solidus half turned and looked at him before answering.

"This is a portal through the chaos. Through it we can travel to any other portal in the world in a matter of moments. We will use it to travel to the portal below the Temple of Alenon. Agamemnon already knows we are coming and will meet us there when we arrive." Vesth chose not to ask any more questions and Rielle/Solidus turned back to the rings. Rielle's arms rose in the air and she spoke strange words. The moonlight that streamed in through the opening behind them twisted and warped and flowed into a single collective pool between Rielle's outstretched hands. The pool grew large, and when it touched Rielle's hands it streamed into the gem at the center of the rings. The gem grew brighter and brighter until it looked as if the moon itself had been transferred into it.

Then the light flowed out into the smaller gems in each ring, filling them with brilliant silver light. After a few seconds, there was a great squeal of metal and the rings began to move. Each ring began to spin on a single point, and each one in a different direction. They spun faster and faster and the gems became streaks of light. Sparks flew from the rings as they spun, causing Tiasia to jump with a squeak. Rielle/Solidus continued to chant, feeding the condensed moonlight into the portal until it was spinning so quickly that it seemed to be a single solid surface. Rielle's arms fell to her sides and she turned and waved.

"Come, we must step through the portal immediately. The moon's power will hold it open, but not for very long." Vesth nodded and started forward. Rielle/Solidus joined him and helped him support Segine. Rielle felt something press against her back and glanced back to see Tiasia clinging to her waist pressing her face tightly against her back. Rielle felt her empty hand pat the girl on the head.

"All will be well little one." Solidus reassured her. They walked up to the portal and Rielle/Solidus propelled them forward, not allowing them time to flinch back. Vesth felt the light wash over him, filling everything with brightness. Then he was stepping out into an identical room to the one they had just left. Except this room was pure white and Agamemnon stood at the other end, a stretcher seemingly floating beside him.

Rielle/Solidus steered them towards the old man, who helped them lift Segine onto the stretcher. Some words passed between Solidus and Agamemnon and then they were moving again. Vesth was finding it hard to concentrate on anything and so he followed Rielle blindly down the halls of the temple until he found himself sitting in the dining hall, Rielle offering him a drink. Vesth thankfully drank what he was given and slowly his mind began to clear. He looked around and saw Tiasia receiving the same drink he had.

"Solidus says the first time through a portal is always difficult." Rielle said. "This will help you clear your head." Tiasia looked around.

"Where are we?" She asked. Rielle smiled and tousled the little girl's hair.

"Somewhere safe."

"What about Segine?" Rielle turned to Vesth with a relieved sigh.

"Agamemnon says that we got him here in time. He will remove the infection and he should recover by morning. The wound will take a few more days to heal, but he will survive it." Vesth nodded and was happy to hear good news for a change.

"Until then, Solidus has asked me to fill you in on what is happening." Rielle stated. Vesth looked up at Rielle.

"What were those creatures that were after us?" Rielle nodded and then looked at Tiasia. Tiasia folded her arms and settled deeper into her chair.

"I am not going anywhere, I want to hear too." Rielle smiled and then turned back to Vesth.

"They are called Nibilus. They were sealed beneath the Serpent Tongue Mountains ages ago, very near the beginning of the world."

"Why were they sealed away?" Tiasia asked. Rielle sat for a moment in thought then answered.

"They were bloodthirsty and corrupted... and they were once humans."

"What?" Vesth asked, sitting up in his seat. Rielle nodded sadly.

"They were once humans. Long ago, when the religion of chaos first came into existence, those who practiced it were weak and at the mercy of those who believed in the Six Deities. So they began to experiment. A demon could not hold a physical form in the world, so they tried to place them inside human hosts. Most hosts died in the process, unable to handle the strain of a demon inside them. Some were corrupted, becoming Nibilus. A few managed to maintain a semblance of their former intelligence. These grew larger and more powerful and were able to control those who had been corrupted. These were named Basilisk." Vesth shivered at the thought that there were worse things than the creatures he had seen on the plains. Rielle continued.

"They, of course, perfected the process and eventually were able to host a demon inside a human body. But there still remained hundreds of Nibilus and dozens of Basilisk. These were taken and sealed in caves beneath the mountains. Now the Telatians have released them, hoping to use them as a mindless army. Completely obedient and subservient." Vesth placed his elbows on the table and laced his fingers together in front of him.

"So, there are hundreds of these things out there?" Rielle shrugged.

"We don't know. There may be hundreds, or there could be thousands. They have spent millennia underground, anything could have happened to them. We don't know if some of them died off or if they multiplied, or if they even can multiply for that matter. Same goes for the Basilisk." Vesth stared at the table top, his chin resting on his hands.

"So they have the element of surprise. We don't know how many there are or where." Rielle shrugged again.

"No, we don't. But we do know their strengths and their weaknesses. They fear light and it can destroy them if they get too close for very long. They are pack hunters, strong together, but alone they are weak. They do not have minds of their own to think, they only have the urge to kill and feed. They must have a Basilisk nearby to control them or they do not know how to act and they turn on one another." Vesth nodded and then stood as he heard the door open and Agamemnon walked into the room.

"It is done. Your friend is resting now. By morning he will be strong enough to stand on his own again. Until then, the rest of you should get some sleep. You have had a long day and you need your rest." Rielle bowed.

"Thank you Agamemnon. We appreciate your hospitality." Agamemnon nodded his head in return.

"The Temple of Alenon is always open to you if you are in need of it." Rielle nodded. "Thank you again. We will go to our rest now. I will let the little one sleep in my room, there is no need for her to be alone in a strange place." Agamemnon nodded and smiled when Tiasia had a look of relief cross her face.

"Then goodnight, your rooms are the same as when last you were here. We will meet here in the morning for break-fast." Rielle bowed again as Agamemnon left the room. When the old priest was gone, Vesth stretched his back.

"I think it is time to turn in for the night." Rielle picked up Tiasia, who was already starting to nod off.

"Can you find your way to your room on your own? Tiasia will be asleep by the time I get to my own room."

"I will not. I could stay awake all night. Really, I am not tired at all." The little girl mumbled tiredly against Rielle's shoulder. Rielle chuckled and Vesth was careful not to smile.

"I can find my way. Be careful with that one though, from

the sounds of things you will be up all night with her." Tiasia tried lifting her hand in the air.

"That's right. All night long with Rielle. We will have a party." The last sentence trailed away as Tiasia dozed off and her hand fell limply to her side. Rielle smiled at the little girl and then walked to the door, which opened for her, and down the dark hall towards her room. Vesth watched them go, half smiling to himself, then left the dining hall to seek his own bed.

Chapter Thirteen

By the time Vesth reached the dining hall the next morning, everyone was already awake and well into their breakfasts. Segine was eating ravenously from several plates at once as Tiasia sat nearby with her own plate of food trying to talk and eat at the same time. Rielle sat across the table and watched as she ate, and Agamemnon sat at the head of the table, seemingly oblivious of his guests.

"Good morning mister Vesth." Tiasia said, stumbling over his name as she spoke around a mouthful of biscuits and a bit of sausage. Vesth noticed a twitch that was almost a smile at the corner of the old Priest's mouth. Vesth waved to the little girl and she went on talking to Segine who merely nodded and continued to eat. Vesth took his seat next to Rielle.

"How are things this morning?" He asked her as he filled his plate from the platters and bowls. Rielle wiped her mouth with a handkerchief.

"Good. Segine remembered most of what happened last night, up until the portal anyway. I told him about his recovery and the Nibilus and he is ready to continue with our journey once breakfast is over." Vesth nodded and started into his food.

"And what is the plan? What is the next part of this journey?" Rielle shrugged.

"I am not one hundred percent sure. Solidus says there is one more person who we need to have join us, but he won't tell me who it is or where we can find them. He says we have to wait until we are back in the Mercury Mountains before he will tell us where to go." Vesth sighed.

"That seems about right." Agamemnon chuckled, not unlike Solidus.

"Solidus does not always reveal everything he knows, but he has good reason. If you knew everything there was to know about what you were going to do next, things would turn out much differently than they should. You might choose not even to proceed if you knew what was going to happen before it did." Vesth paused for a moment.

"Does Solidus see the future?" Agamemnon shrugged.

"The exact extent of what Solidus sees is known only to Solidus. But he does not see the future, per se. He sees how everything that is in balance affects everything else. He can see the consequences of a given choice or action. Once a choice has been made, more possibilities open to his vision. The trick is to learn to wait until the critical moment a choice is made to decide how to react." Vesth thought about that while he slowly chewed his food.

"When I first met Solidus, he told me he wouldn't help me unless a certain choice was made." Rielle interjected. "Is that why?" Agamemnon nodded.

"Yes. He could see that, if High Priest Borsa were to reject the demon that offered to take him as host, this entire series of events could have been avoided. If balance could right itself without his intervention, he would let things happen as they should. In most cases when something puts the world out of balance, it fixes itself. Something rises up to balance what fell. But in some few cases, such as yours, someone else must help tip the scales."

"Why are we here then?" Vesth asked, suddenly finding that his food was not very appetizing. Agamemnon glanced at him.

"There are... predictions. Long ago, even before Solidus was born, The balance mages came together in Alenon and attempted to look into the future to see how the world would end. What they found were endless possibilities. But they did find that the end of the world would be one of two things. The first would be that the world would achieve absolute balance within itself and would never be threatened by destruction again." Segine coughed once and then spoke.

"I do not mean to interrupt venerated one, but how is achieving balance an end to the world?" Agamemnon chuckled.

"In the sense that the world would cease to exist, it is not an end. However, it would mean that the chaos is cleansed and the Six Deities could come and go to our world as they wished without upsetting the balance or their power. There would no longer be need for faithfulness or piety. There would be no hunger, no war, no poverty. Everything would be in harmony." Segine sat back in his chair, nodding.

"I understand."

"What about the second way the world ends?" Tiasia asked.

"This is not really a discussion for young children." Segine told her. Tiasia folded her arms across her chest and stuck her tongue out at him. Segine sputtered, looking for a way to scold her, but Agamemnon held up a hand.

"It is alright, Segine, She needs to hear as much as the rest of you." Segine nodded and sat back in his chair, carefully avoiding eye contact with Tiasia.

"So what is the second way?" Vesth asked. Agamemnon gave Vesth a sober look.

"The complete unbalancing of the world. Everything returning to chaos." Everyone was quiet for several minutes until Rielle finally spoke.

"All predictions end this way?" Agamemnon shook his head.

"The predictions showed them only that these were the two ways that the world would end. The way these ends were achieved were numberless. The Balance Mages sifted through the endless possibilities for years until a few thousand appeared to be the most likely ends. These were written and passed down to every balance mage after them to watch for the choices that would end the world. As the years passed by, more and more of the predictions were crossed out as their choices came and went with no conclusion. There are only some few hundred left. Now that Master Solidus is the only surviving Balance Mage, it falls to him to watch for all the predictions." Rielle swallowed hard. Vesth watched her for a moment then turned back to the old priest.

"So, we are one of the predictions?" Agamemnon shrugged again.

"Truth be told, we won't know until it reaches its conclusion. However, up until now everything fits. 'A war spawned by chaos as the Blood Moon Cycle draws near. An alliance of powers to fight the chaos and fear. A deal made with a terror for power. A knife in the back at a desperate hour. A careful dragon wields his blade. A strong life force is heaven bade'..." "Careful Agamemnon." Solidus's voice was strong, nearly erasing Rielle's completely. Agamemnon bowed in his chair.

"Yes, of course Master Solidus. Please forgive me, I forgot myself." Rielle/Solidus nodded and then Rielle's eyes returned to normal. Agamemnon took a moment to compose himself.

"As you can see some things fit the prediction, such as the war near the time of the Blood Moon Cycle. Some have tried to force predictions to end the world before, but they have thus far failed. But, unlike other predictions, this one cannot be faked. The only ones who can foresee the time of a Blood Moon Cycle is a balance mage or the Six Deities. The priest of the chaos order and the demons can guess, but they cannot know when the cycle will be. In that we have an advantage." Vesth sat quietly thinking.

"If this is a prediction, is it one that ends good or bad?" Tiasia asked. Agamemnon smiled.

"Smart girl. This prediction, if that is indeed what it is, is somewhat different than most others. This prediction can end both ways." Segine leaned forward.

"How is that possible?" Agamemnon shrugged.

"I do not know. I am not a balance mage, I do not see how the world turns. But this prediction can end differently depending on what choices are made. I cannot speak of them, for that would influence what choices you make now and could have drastic affects in the future. Just follow the guidance of Solidus and you will come out of this alright. Remember that." A bell tolled somewhere inside the temple. Agamemnon looked around.

"Is it really so late? I did not realize we had been here so long. It is time for you all to go. I will open the portal to return you all to Solidus's home in the Mercury Mountains. Solidus will tell you what you need to do from there." Rielle stood from the table and the others followed. "We are ready." Agamemnon stood as well.

"Then follow me to the portal. And good luck to you all."

* * *

Rielle sat in a high backed chair against one wall. Vesth sat on a wooden stool beside her, and they both watched as Tiasia sat with Segine before the fireplace, asking about what it was like to be a knight. Rielle half smiled as she watched, remembering when she had been young and curious of such things. The fire burned brightly and easily warmed the small hut. When they had returned through the portal they had found a fresh layer of snow on the ground and had quickly retreated into the warmth of the hut.

"Do you know what we are to do?" Vesth asked her. She shook her head.

"Solidus told me that we must wait until nightfall. Beyond that, I do not know." Vesth nodded slowly.

"Then we wait." Rielle nodded.

"If you wish, Solidus says there is good hunting in the forest by the cliffs. It could keep you occupied until tonight." Vesth shook his head.

"No, I do not think so. I was never much good with a bow, and the time spent tracking prey could be better spent training or meditating." Rielle smiled.

"You spend so much time thinking on your training and your duties. Have you ever done something just for fun?" Vesth looked at Rielle as if she had suggested something very strange. Rielle stared in disbelief for a moment and then laughed. Vesth continued to watch Rielle.

"I fail to see what is so amusing." He stated. Rielle laughed harder and it caught Tiasia's attention.

"What is so funny?" She asked, jumping up and rushing to Rielle's side. Rielle calmed herself and whispered into the little girl's ear. Tiasia listened for a moment and then fell over in fits of giggling. Rielle laughed again as Segine walked to Vesth's side.

"What is so funny?" He asked. Vesth shrugged.

"I am yet to understand." Both men watched as Rielle and Tiasia giggled and laughed until Rielle gained enough control to speak again.

"Sir Segine, have you ever done something simply for the fun of it?" The big knight gave her a strange look.

"I am not sure I understand what you mean." Tiasia scoffed.

"A game, you silly. Have you ever played a game?" The little girl looked at both men. Segine shrugged.

"When I was very young perhaps." Tiasia and Rielle looked at Vesth. Vesth shifted uncomfortably.

"I have never understood the need to play games before. I

do not see any benefit to be gained from it." Rielle stared in surprise. Tiasia's eyes widened.

"You have never played a single game before?" Vesth shook his head and Tiasia's eyes widened further.

"You never played hide-and-seek? I see? Chase and tag?" Vesth shook his head to all of them.

"Have you ever even had a snowball fight?" Rielle asked. Vesth again shook his head. "*That is just criminal.*" Solidus commented. Rielle shook her head.

"And you Sir Segine?" The big knight shrugged.

"When I was very young, the other children of my father's manor often played such games. I tried to play chase and tag once, but my father caught me and I was put back to my studies." Tiasia shook her head and placed her hands on her hips.

"That is sad. We have to play, right now." Without waiting for permission, Tiasia grabbed Segine's hand and dragged him towards the door. Unsure of what else to do, the knight followed her without trouble. Rielle stood and motioned to Vesth.

"Come on Vesth, it is more fun if there is more than three people." Vesth looked at Rielle as he stood, a little shocked.

"You mean to indulge this young girl? Are there not more important things to be focusing on?" Rielle frowned.

"At the moment? No." Vesth continued to stare.

"But what is the point of such a frivolous activity?" Rielle laughed.

"To be frivolous of course. Come now, even my cousin has played chase and tag before, and he is High King. I do not think it would be beneath you to play." Vesth looked at the ground looking for an argument. Rielle placed her hands on her hips.

"If you must think of it as something other than play, think of it as mastering the art of retreat." Vesth glanced at Rielle and sighed.

"Very well, what are the rules of this exercise?" Rielle shook her head in amazement. "One person is 'It' everyone else runs away from them. If the person who is it tags you, then you are 'It'. Then you have to catch someone else and tag them 'It'. Make sense?" Vesth shook his head sullenly.

"No, but I understand."

"Chase and tag? I remember playing that with the young children around the temple ages ago." Solidus mentioned. *"Except I think we played it where everyone chased whoever was 'It'... come to think of it, I seemed to get picked as 'It' quite frequently."* Rielle suppressed her giggle and shoed Vesth out of the hut and onto the snow covered area outside, closing the door behind her. Vesth blinked in the bright light for a moment and then glanced down. Tiasia ran up full speed and touched Vesth's arm and immediately turned and ran in the opposite direction, sliding in the snow.

"Your It!" She yelled excitedly. Rielle smiled and danced out of reach when Vesth turned around.

"Now you have to tag someone else." She said, then she gave him a sly look. "If you can." She giggled girlishly and ran out into the open. Vesth looked around for a moment and caught sight of Segine, standing ankle deep in the snow. The knight shrugged. Vesth sighed again and set out after Tiasia.

* * *

Vesth hid behind one corner of the hut, a cold snowball

numbing one of his hands. Early on, the game of chase and tag had somehow become an all out war of icy projectiles. Vesth had quickly learned that chasing after Tiasia and trying to hit her with a snowball was a pointless endeavor. The little girl was deceptively fast and she was such a small target that trying to hit her on the run was nearly impossible.

Vesth peaked around the corner and saw Segine trying to sneak from the hut to the place where they had the horses tied. Vesth quickly stepped out and hurled his snowball. Segine noticed just in time to turn and take the snowball straight in the face. The big knight jumped and hurriedly wiped the stinging snow from his cheeks. Vesth was about to announce his victory over the knight when a snowball zipped past him, inches from his head, and another hit him squarely in the back. He jumped around the corner of the hut and peaked back around the other way. Two more snowballs flew at him and he barely pulled his face out of the way in time.

Vesth hugged the wall thinking carefully when he realized Segine was still to his back. He turned around and watched the big knight charge at him with a battle cry, a melon sized snowball held above his head. Vesth shivered at the thought of how cold he was going to be in a moment and then watched as the knight took a snowball in the ribs and another to the face. The knight dropped his arms to protect his face, promptly dropping the large snowball on top of his head. Vesth tried not to laugh as the knight dropped to the ground, wriggling around, trying to get the snow out of his tunic. Vesth smiled and then waved his hand.

"This way Sir Segine, hide here." Segine crawled across the

ground, another two snowballs flying over his back, and slid up against the wall next to Vesth.

"What was that?" He asked, wiping the last of the snow off of his face. Vesth shook his head.

"I don't know, but I think the girls have made an alliance against us." Segine patted his wet tunic.

"Well, whatever it is they are doing seems to be working." Vesth nodded.

"Indeed it does." Vesth looked around the corner again and watched as Rielle and Tiasia rose up from behind a wall of snow they had constructed and lobbed more snowballs at his exposed head. He pulled his head out of the way and watched the snowballs sail past.

"Where are they?" Segine asked. "There isn't any cover over there that I am aware of." Vesth gave a short laugh.

"There wasn't any cover, until they packed the snow together into a wall." Segine scratched his chin.

"That is pretty smart." Vesth nodded.

"They have obviously done this before." Segine shrugged.

"Don't look at me, this is my first snowball fight. It almost never snows in the plains." Vesth nodded.

"I have seen snow before many times, but I never had occasion to have a fight with it." Segine chuckled heartily.

"Then we are both at a large disadvantage. What should we do?" Vesth thought for a moment.

"You go out and distract them, I will run around the other way and chase them from their hiding place." Segine nodded.

"I will go to my death with glory." Vesth turned to leave and then paused.

"Oh, and Segine." Vesth said, doing his best not to smile.

"You may want to cover your face." The knight grumbled and Vesth made his way to the other side of the house. When he got there he motioned to Segine who ran out into the open, arms across his face. Snowballs immediately started flying. Vesth took a few breaths and then dashed out around the hut and headed straight for the wall of snow.

Half way Tiasia spotted him and pointed him out with a little squeal. The snowballs were now flying at Vesth and he did his best to dodge them while he ran. He got close to them and jumped at their hiding place, landing face first in the snow. Both of them jumped and ran, giggling all the way. Vesth jumped up and wiped the snow from his face. He immediately saw that the girls had been stockpiling snowballs, making them and leaving them in neat little stacks behind their wall. He picked up two and threw them in quick succession at the fleeing girls.

The first flew wide, but the second flew straight at Rielle. Vesth smiled at this and then frowned as Rielle turned and caught the snowball in mid air. Even from that distance, Vesth could see that her eyes had turned silver.

"I hate to interrupt while things are going so well." Solidus said, a faint smile touching Rielle lips.

"But the sun will be setting soon and we will need to move out. It would be wise for you to go inside and dry yourselves by the fire and pack your things before we leave." Rielle's eyes returned to normal and she looked at the snowball in her hand, debating with herself on whether or not to throw it. Eventually she shrugged and dropped it.

"I think going in to the fire would be wise. My hands are very cold." She said.

"Mine too." Tiasia agreed. They all headed back towards the hut and Vesth fell in next to Segine, brushing the snow off of himself. He looked up at the house and down to the ground, then quickly back up to the house. Being careful not to let the two girls see Vesth nudged Segine and motioned towards the hut. Segine followed his eyes and saw the snow piled up on the roof just above the door. Segine looked back down at Vesth with a sly wink and they walked to the door.

Vesth walked inside and Segine motioned for the two girls to go before him. As they got to the door, Segine and Vesth both rammed the walls with their shoulders and Segine jumped out of the way as the snow cascaded down off the roof onto the heads of the two girls. Both gasped as they were covered with the cold snow. Segine threw his head back laughing and Vesth shook slightly, suppressing his own laughter. Tiasia turned with a little war cry and jumped at the knight, grabbing him around the neck shoving hands full of snow down his back. The big knight gasped, but continued to laugh and picked the little girl up off the ground, wriggling and fighting, and took her inside to the fire. Rielle followed him in and wrinkled her nose in a scowl, pointing at Vesth.

"I will get you later." She stated. Vesth smiled and Rielle smiled back before going to the fire to warm her hands. By the time they had all dried off and packed, the sun had set well below the horizon.

"It is time to go." Rielle stated. They got their packs settled on their shoulders and made their way out the door and down the path that led to the forest below. When they came to the cave, Rielle turned away and headed down a steep ravine on a path that had almost completely faded away. They followed the path until it met a second ravine and turned to follow it. The way was steep and rocky and they all lost their footing more than a few times before they reached the top. They came out on top of a low saddle in the mountains and Vesth looked around.

He didn't like what he saw. Even though the moon was only a sliver less than full, the trees around them swallowed what little light it gave. The leaves were slick and so dark that they were almost black. A few black pines were scattered amongst the other trees, adding a sense of death to the forest. Vesth looked back the way they had come. He could see both ravines and the path that led to Solidus's hut.

"Wow." Tiasia stated pointing at the Hermit Peak. From that distance they could not see the hut on top of the mountain, but the peak itself stood out in bright contrast to the rest of the Mercury Mountains. It was high and almost perfectly round at the top, and it seemed to glow with other-worldly light as the moonlight reflected off of the fallen snow.

"Keep on your toes." Solidus stated, having taken over Rielle's body. "We have left the protected path and are now in the wilds of the Mercury Mountains. Out here there are things beyond your comprehension. If you see or hear anything, you tell me. None of you are capable of fighting off anything we might come across in here so don't try." When they had all nodded their agreement Rielle/Solidus nodded once.

"Good. Follow closely. We have a long way to go tonight." No one argued and they all fell into a line and started out into the blackened trees.

15

❧

Chapter Fourteen

Very quickly they discovered that the very air in the trees seemed to sap at every happy thought. After only minutes of being among the trees they were settled over by a depressed silence. Many times Rielle motioned everyone to stop and wait for several moments before they continued their gloomy hike. They mainly stayed below the timberline, hiding among the dark trees. Only once did they cross over a bare ridgeline, and Rielle forced them to stop and wait for a long few minutes before she rushed them over and back into the trees.

"What is it we are trying to avoid?" Vesth asked, as they stopped yet again. Rielle's eyes darted back and forth among the shadows. Then she leaned back and whispered carefully into his ear.

"There are some things here that hunt mainly at night. Solidus says he can fight them, but he doesn't know that he could protect everyone while he is inside the confines of my body. It is best just to avoid them altogether." Vesth nodded and didn't say anything else, his own eyes now watching every shadow. By the time Rielle finally called a stop, the sky was starting to lighten above the mountains to the east. Rielle looked carefully around the corner of a cliff and then led them out to a semi clear area before an enormous cave entrance. They stood silently for several seconds before Solidus spoke through Rielle.

"No one move. No one act or react in any way." Vesth shuffled nervously. Then a faint scrape was heard within the cavern and Rielle drew Solidus's sword and deflected a thin black dart. A figure shot from the cave, sword raised overhead, and struck at Rielle. Rielle easily intercepted the blow and was able to turn and let the attacker run by. Vesth's hand fell to his sword and he watched Segine do the same, flinching at the wound in his shoulder, but Rielle held out a hand and Solidus spoke.

"Leave your swords as they are." Vesth reluctantly let go of his sword and turned to inspect their attacker more closely. In the dark of the early morning he could not make out much. The figure before them was clad all in black and had a black hood drawn up over their face. A few locks of jet black hair cascaded from the hood and down either shoulder. The sword they wielded was a long, thin, double-edged blade with an ornate cross guard and serrations along the bottom five inches. Rielle/Solidus smiled.

"You have improved your technique from the last time we met, Nysisset." The figure grunted slightly and then spoke with an almost irresistibly sweet voice.

"It seems to me that you were only a wizened old hermit when last we met. And now look at you, surrounded by people and inhabiting a new young body." Rielle felt slightly angry at this mystery woman. Solidus merely chuckled.

"I can assure you, I am only a guest in this body. My own body is no longer available to me. As for those who you see with me, they are here out of necessity, not for their companionship." The mystery woman laughed lightly, though Vesth felt as if he could hear it twisting as it left her throat.

"Old hermit, why did you come to this place? It is risky for you to come without your full strength, especially with those whom you would have to defend as well. Your new host could burn up if you're not careful." Rielle felt a pang in the pit of her stomach, but Solidus filled her with calm to reassure her.

"We are here to see your master, Nysisset. Khornal is expecting me." The woman called Nysisset lowered her sword.

"His Greatness is very irked with you, Solidus. Your predictions are causing him no end of trouble." Rielle/Solidus shrugged.

"He is bound by balance, as are the other five. And he knows as well as the others that this is not my doing. His frustrations will simply have to be directed elsewhere. Now, we have little time to spare, Nysisset, so if you would be so kind as to lead the way, we can get out of here as quickly as possible." The woman Nysisset finally sheathed her sword and pulled back her hood. Vesth was shocked. Nysisset had deep violet eyes and nearly perfect features. A simple black tattoo started on either side of her eyes, crossed her cheeks and traveled down the side of her neck. The rest of her shining black hair, no longer confined by the black hood, now fell around her shoulders and down her back.

"As you wish, Silver Mage. I don't know what you want

here, but I will be much happier when you are gone." Rielle/Solidus smiled and half bowed.

"Of course." He replied, Then Rielle's eyes returned to normal. Rielle returned Solidus's sword to its scabbard and stepped aside for Nysisset. The woman in black glided gracefully by, her nose in the air, and led them into the cave. Vesth would not have believed it possible that anything could be darker than the forest outside. But the inside of the cave was black as pitch and even more depressing than it had been outside.

Rielle conjured up a small golden ball in her hand to light their way and held it high overhead. Even as bright as her light was, it still did not reach to the ceiling. Nysisset glanced back with a smug look and continued deeper into the ground. Soon everyone could smell the stench of death and decay rising up from passages below them. Rielle wrinkled her nose and Tiasia made a face, but Vesth and Segine acted as if they smelled nothing. They walked for almost a mile under the ground, deeper and deeper until they came to a cavern that dwarfed the passage they had been in and swallowed Rielle's light almost completely. Nysisset dropped to one knee just inside.

"Oh Great Khornal, Lord of the Mercury Mountains, Solidus the Silver Mage wishes to have an audience." The echoes made it nearly impossible to make out the last words she spoke. There were several moments of nothing as the echoes faded away to silence. Then they heard a soft rasping noise and suddenly flames burst into life all over the cavern. Rielle stared in amazement. The entire cave was filled with gold of every size, shape, and description. Coins, statues, weapons, and more lay in mountainous heaps in a room big enough to hold the castle at Terramine.

"The Silver Mage is welcomed into my hall. Let him and the others through." The voice was low and smooth. Nysisset bowed her head then stood and led them around the piles of gold towards the other end of the room. Tiasia stared, open mouthed at the riches around them.

"Will wonders never cease?" She asked. Rielle chuckled nervously.

"No, little one, They will not." They rounded a particularly large pile of gold coins and suddenly they were standing in a barren grey expanse of stone. Darkness surrounded them on all sides and a bone chilling shiver washed over everyone. Rielle took an extra step and bowed. Solidus spoke.

"Lord Khornal, It has been a long time since our last meeting." Silence reigned for several moments, even the echoes being swallowed by the darkness. Then there was a sharp rasp and a colossal dragon's head slid from the darkness, scraps of flesh barely clinging to its skeletal frame.

"It has been very long indeed Silver Mage, what brings you to my domain?" The undead dragon craned his neck and casually looked at the others in the group as Rielle stood straight. "The vacant expressions of awe and fear never cease to amuse me." He stated. Rielle glanced behind her and saw both men staring unashamedly at the creature and Tiasia was shivering in terror. Rielle scowled inwardly when she saw Nysisset's look of smug amusement. Solidus spoke again.

"Fear is your domain, it does not surprise me." The undead dragon turned back to Rielle with a chuckle.

"For a follower of my sister, you show a spectacular lack of care for others." Solidus smiled.

"On the contrary, I care a great deal for others. But they must have their own experiences, I will not keep that from them. Besides, this is an experience most humans will never have the... pleasure of living through." The undead dragon chuckled again.

"We both know you are only barely human. All of you Alenon mages ceased to be truly human when my sister gave you eternal youth." Rielle/Solidus shrugged.

"Perhaps so, it is not my place to argue with my Patroness. However, at the present, we have more pressing matters to discuss. And as grand as you are, Great Khornal, I think it would be easier for everyone if you came down to our level." Khornal growled.

"You presume that I should take the form of a human?" Tiasia whimpered and hid her face in Vesth's side. Rielle/ Solidus smiled.

"You could take the form of a cow if you would prefer." Khornal glared at Rielle for a few seconds and then burst into deep, rumbling laughter. Solidus chuckled and the undead dragon dissolved into a black mist that fell to the floor. The mist rebuilt itself into the form of a slim man in black clothing and hair so dark that even Nysisset's hair seemed brighter by comparison. The man laughed for a few seconds more before speaking.

"Your wit is as sharp as ever, Solidus. It is too bad that you will not leave my sister to come serve me." Rielle/Solidus shrugged.

"I am devoted to my Deity, and I don't think she would let

you have me anyway. I am not quite that much of a nuisance just yet." Khornal nodded and waved one hand, a black throne materialized behind him and he sat down.

"Too bad. But as you said before, we have more important matters to discuss. What has brought you here?" Rielle/Solidus nodded.

"I have come because of the predictions." Khornal groaned, covering his face with one hand and summoning a glass of wine into his other.

"Again? Has the soldier again set fire to something else you wish me to douse?" Khornal motioned to Vesth who did his best to remain steady. Solidus chuckled.

"No, Vesth has been careful since then. I am here for the final companion of the prediction. The last one to join us before we can begin to prepare for a confrontation with Borsa." Khornal scowled.

"I dislike that man. There is no honor in his evil, only Will bent on Destruction. I wish I could get my hands on him." He crushed his wine glass, which shattered into a thousand needles of black mist before reforming in his hand again. "I guess I will have to settle with simply sending one of my servants with you to deal with him. Of course, how you plan to take them outside the confines of the Mercury Mountains eludes me. All of my evil and followers are sealed here." Rielle/Solidus nodded.

"Indeed, but if you were to seal your servant to me, they could leave the Mercury Mountains without harm." Khornal sipped at his wine and tapped on his chin.

"Now that is thinking, isn't it? Yes, I suppose I could do that. Of course they would have to be bound to your soul, the girl you are in is strong, but her simple human frame would shatter if physically bound." Rielle/Solidus nodded.

"This I know. Are you willing to part with a servant?" Khornal nodded with a wave.

"Anyone you need. You know my servants, which one do you need to fill the prediction?" Rielle/Solidus shook his head, half smiling.

"I don't think you will be pleased, Khornal. The prediction clearly states that there will be an 'Alliance of powers to fight the chaos and fear' and of them, the last, is 'a being both fear and angel as one'. Your 'Angel of Death' is the only one who can fit this role." Khornal sat up straight, his wine glass disappearing.

"So you are telling me that the only one you will take is..." Rielle/Solidus nodded. "Nysisset, the Mercury Mountain's Angel of Death."

* * *

"Absolutely not! I refuse to be demeaned in this way." Nysisset complained. Khornal glanced at her from his throne.

"You would deny the wish of your master?" He asked her. Nysisset sputtered slightly. "No my lord, but surely he could choose someone else. There are hundreds of your servants that would gladly take up this request."

"But none of them would fit the prediction." Solidus stated. Nysisset glared at Rielle.

"I couldn't care less about your stupid predictions. I won't let you take me." Nysisset placed one hand on her sword.

"That is enough out of you, Nysisset." Khornal said in a low and menacing voice. Nysisset flinched and turned back to Khornal and dropped to one knee.

"Don't be a fool. You are skilled with a blade, but Solidus could beat you without batting an eye. And this is my command, you will follow Solidus to the end of this prediction even if it kills you." Nysisset's lip trembled and she bowed her head.

"As you speak, Great Master. I will do as you have commanded." Khornal nodded once. "Good. Now, Solidus, you know how this works." Rielle/Solidus nodded and Rielle turned and took the few steps to Nysisset's side. Rielle placed one hand on Nysisset's head and her eyes returned to normal.

"Solidus is ready, Great Khornal. He is sorry he cannot speak directly, but he fears that if he is not completely separate from me the binding will not succeed." Khornal nodded and stood, his black throne disappearing.

"Very well, I hereby release this soul from my charge and bind it to the soul of the Balance Mage, Pravin Solidus, to do with as he sees fit." Tendrils of darkness spread from Khornal and he directed them with his hands. The tendrils flowed across the room and filled Nysisset who gasped with the sudden invasion of her body. Her violet eyes lightened until they were a pale shadow of their former color. Then the tendrils of darkness flowed out of Nysisset's eyes and entered Rielle's. Rielle stood still and made no sound as the energy filled her. And as quickly as it started, it ended. The tendrils left both women and returned to Khornal.

"It is done Solidus. This creature is now yours to command as you wish." Rielle's eyes turned silver and Solidus spoke.

"Indeed. I thank you for your cooperation." Khornal waved a hand.

"It is not like I had much choice in the matter. Go and do

what must be done, and if possible I would like to have my servant back in one peace when you are through with her. For being a follower of the light, you have an unusual reputation for being brutally unhelpful when you feel the need. Tell my sister I send my love, If you have the chance." Rielle/Solidus bowed. "I will. Farewell, Khornal." Khornal waved again and turned into a cloud of black mist that disappeared into the blackness beyond where the light of the fires could not touch. Rielle rose from her bow and turned to Nysisset, her eyes returning to normal.

"You may stand, Nysisset. Solidus says you can lead us to a cave that passes under the mountains and back to the peak where he lives." Nysisset stood slowly, her violet eyes now almost clear.

"Why must this be my fate? Why must I walk in the servitude of a child of light?" Rielle sighed and was quiet for several moments before speaking.

"You can make your fate anything you wish. As for being in servitude, Solidus says you are not his servant. You are merely our companion now. When everything comes to its end you may return here if you so desire. Now please, lead the way." Nysisset stood and looked at Rielle. "It is not proper to walk ahead of one's master, even if he is imprisoned inside the body of a useless human." Rielle carefully checked her anger.

"Be that as it may, you will lead us through the caves. Tiasia." The little girl peaked out from behind Vesth and looked at Rielle.

"Yes?" She asked timidly. Rielle motioned to her and she quickly ran to her side.

"Tiasia, this is our new friend, Nysisset. Hold her hand

and have her show you how we can get back to Master Solidus's home." Tiasia nodded and ran to Nysisset's side and took hold of one of her hands. Nysisset looked down at the little girl with a dumbfounded expression. "Come on miss Nysisset, let's go." Tiasia said and dragged Nysisset off, back through the room full of gold. Nysisset quickly recovered and tried to remove the little girl from her hand, but could not, no matter what she tried.

"It would be best to give in and just let her hold your hand." Rielle stated as she and the others followed. Nysisset glared at Rielle and, after a few more moments of struggle, gave in and just held Tiasia's hand. Vesth made his way to Rielle's side and spoke.

"Was that truly the Deity of Evil we just met?" Rielle nodded, hiding her own shock and fear.

"Yes. Necrotic Dracolich Khornal, Deity of Evil."

"How is that possible?" Segine asked from behind them.

"I thought the six Deities lived in the heaven realm and never ventured down here to interfere." Rielle nodded.

"They don't, but Khornal is a little different. When Alenon was destroyed, all those who followed and worshiped the Deity of Evil were sealed in the Mercury Mountains to maintain balance. But the only way to keep them sealed here indefinitely was for Khornal to physically come to this realm and guard the mountains. Because of this, he is now bound here and cannot return to the heaven realm until the world is in complete balance... Or so Solidus tells me." Vesth and Segine shared a glance and both nodded.

"If you fools are done whispering amongst yourselves back there, we have places to go." Nysisset said irritably, Tiasia still attached to her hand. Now that they were away from Khornal and his main cave, Tiasia was slowly returning to her normal self. She bounced and wiggled and asked an unending stream of questions which Nysisset pointedly ignored. They turned and went down a small path and followed it for several minutes before coming to a dead end.

"Are you sure this is the way?" Tiasia asked. Rielle could see Nysisset's annoyance. "Yes, little girl, I am sure." Tiasia bounced happily.

"You can call me Tiasia." Nysisset groaned and Rielle smiled.

"We will need a coin to pass beyond this point and return to the Hermit's Peak." Rielle's smile fell and looked to Segine and Vesth. Both shook their heads. Nysisset sighed in exasperation.

"Don't any of you carry money with you?" They shook their heads.

"Here's some." Tiasia stated happily, holding up a large gold coin with her empty hand. "Where did you get that?" Rielle asked in surprise. Tiasia looked back at Rielle, eyes wide and innocent.

"There were great big piles of gold in the room back there, didn't anyone notice?" Segine burst out laughing and was quickly silenced by Vesth. Nysisset looked at Tiasia in shock.

"You stole gold from Khornal's horde!?" Tiasia shrugged.

"He wasn't using it." Rielle laughed and Solidus took control of her body.

"It is all well, Nysisset. Even Khornal cannot remain angry at an innocent like her for long. Besides, I think he would be rather amused at the thought that he was stolen from so easily beneath his notice. Take the coin and lead on, there is still much to be done." Nysisset grumbled and took the coin from Tiasia as Rielle's eyes returned to normal. Nysisset pressed the coin against the wall and spoke a few words and both the coin and wall disappeared. They walked for a few more minutes and found themselves in a familiar setting.

"This is the cave we went through to get to Alenon." Vesth said in amazement. "How did we get here so quickly?" Nysisset sniffed.

"It is none of your business."

"There are many passages like this one that lead to places all over in the mountains. But they only work one way, that is why Solidus led us over the tops of the mountains to get to Khornal's cave in the first place." Rielle smiled at Nysisset after explaining. "Come, Solidus says we should rest and head out tomorrow morning." They all nodded and left the cave and made their way up the mountain path to the peak just as the sun rose in the east.

They entered Solidus's hut and made a simple breakfast before Tiasia curled up in a chair beside Nysisset and went to sleep. Nysisset sat rigidly, unsure of what to do, and simply stared at one wall. Rielle smiled and lifted Tiasia into her arms, carrying her to a bed roll beside the fire and laying her down. Then she returned to Nysisset and sat in a chair across from her.

"Tell me about yourself." She said. Nysisset looked at her blankly.

"I am not important, I am only here to finish my charge." Rielle smiled.

"You sound like Vesth. If you ask him, he will tell you he

is simply here to fulfill his duty as a soldier. But once you get to know him, you find he is a kind and simple person." They looked across the room where both Vesth and Segine sat honing the edges of their swords.

"We are to be companions." Rielle continued. "I would know more about you." Nysisset looked away from Rielle.

"I am sure Solidus could tell you everything you want to know." Rielle nodded.

"He could, but I want to hear it from you." Nysisset glanced at Rielle through the corner of her eye.

"Why? What difference does it make where you hear it from?" Rielle smiled again.

"You don't know this yet, but before I started to learn under Master Solidus, and before he saved my life by destroying his own body, I was one of the top Ambassadors in Hortaal." Nysisset turned to face Rielle.

"An ambassador?" Rielle nodded.

"Yes. And in my many years of being ambassador I have learned a few things that make me quite good at it. One thing I have learned is that if you want accurate information about anything, it is best to go to the source. Solidus could tell me all about you, but his words would be tainted by his personal opinion. If I hear it from you, it will only be the truth, not someone else's opinions." Nysisset eyed Rielle carefully.

"Perhaps you are not as dim witted as you seemed to be. Very well, But I will only speak of myself if you will provide me with the story of how you got to this point." Rielle nodded.

"I agree, and you should be told of what has happened up

to this point anyway." Nysisset settled back in her chair a little more comfortably.

"You may begin at your whim." Rielle nodded and started at the beginning.

16

Chapter Fifteen

Nysisset sat in the early morning hours before the dimly burning fire. Rielle and Tiasia were asleep not far away and a loud snore came from across the room where Vesth and Segine had made their beds. Nysisset's violet eyes glowed with reflected fire light as she stared into the small dancing flames.

"You should be sleeping." Nysisset jumped as the voice spoke. Vesth stepped silently into the small circle of light cast by the fire.

"We will be setting out in a few hours, you should rest before we go." Nysisset sniffed self importantly. *'How did he sneak up on me without my notice?'*

"Shouldn't you be following your own advice?" She asked. Vesth shrugged.

"I am a soldier, I was raised to live on very few hours of sleep. Besides, someone should check the horses before daylight." Nysisset turned back to the flames.

"I do not need to sleep." She stated stubbornly.

"Yes, you do. But if you do not wish to do so, then it is not my place to tell you that you must." Vesth turned and made his way to the door. He pulled open the lock and pushed the door open quietly.

"Just keep in mind that you will be riding with me until we can acquire more horses. I don't fancy trying to hold you in place if you fall asleep in the saddle. And as little as I yet know of you, I think you would appreciate my 'help' about as much as I would." With this, Vesth slipped out the door and shut it silently behind him. Nysisset frowned and settled deeper into her chair as the thought of Vesth having to hold her up in a saddle filled her mind. Her frown deepened.

"I will not let myself be assisted by a human." She muttered and finally closed her eyes to sleep. Vesth walked lazily towards the horses, snow crunching beneath his feet. He could see where their game had taken place the day before, footprints scattered aimlessly across the ground. He checked his horse and then made sure that they were all taken care of. He broke the ice that had formed in the small watering trough and then turned back towards the hut. He took a few steps and then, on a whim, turned and headed for the path down the mountain.

He walked slowly, looking up at the stars and the moon, taking his time as he thought. When he found himself standing before the small cave, he scratched his chin in thought then went inside and sat down beside the cold fire pit.

"Speak your mind Vesth." Vesth looked up to see the semi-solid image of Solidus before him. Vesth sighed.

"I do not know what it is you see in this new companion you have found for us." Solidus smiled and sat opposite the fire pit.

"Nysisset is strong willed, and she will be bitter about this for some time to come. Once she has accepted it however, she will be an invaluable ally. Just give her time, she will come around. Even as a servant of Khornal, Nysisset has great potential for kindness and caring locked away inside her, waiting to come out." Vesth nodded.

"If you say so, master Solidus." Solidus chuckled.

"Perhaps one day you too will come around and accept your own task. You do not need to think of everything in terms of duty and responsibility. There are times when you must do what you feel, not simply follow through with what you are told is your duty." Vesth bowed his head. "All I have is my duty." Solidus nodded.

"Someday, you will have something different to fight for. Something stronger and far more important than mere duty." Vesth shook his head.

"Only my duty matters." Solidus stood.

"For now that is enough. But when you are ready, that will change." Vesth looked back up at Solidus.

"Go back and get some rest, Vesth. We have a long way to go once it gets light." Vesth nodded and Solidus faded away. Vesth stayed seated before the fire pit for a few minutes more before standing and making his way back up the mountain. By the time he reached the hut, the sky in the east was beginning to lighten. He quickly stepped inside and laid back down on his bed roll. He noticed that Nysisset had finally gone to sleep, her head lolled to one side. With a nod, Vesth took a deep breath and relaxed, closing his eyes and settling himself down to rest.

* * *

Keliter Dona Sungotan stood before the High Priest Borsa's door, watching four figures draped in black cloaks as they waited for admittance.

"Keliter," Came the call from inside. "You may let them in now." Keliter bowed his head in acknowledgment.

"As your grace commands." He took hold of one of the large double doors and pulled it open, stepping aside to let the figures pass. Once all were inside, Keliter followed them in, pulling the door shut behind him. Once the latch had clicked shut he turned his back to the door and stood silently, dutifully waiting for a command from his master.

The four figures formed a semi-circle around the high priest who stood by the altar at the head of the room, staring into a perfect crystal sphere.

"It is good that you all have accepted my summons." The high priest said quietly. He turned to face his guests and Keliter averted his eyes for a moment. The high priest had become pale and thin over the past few weeks. When Keliter had asked about his health, the priest had simply said it was a necessary sacrifice. Now it was difficult to look at him without feeling a pang of pity for the man.

"Some few days from now our plans will come to fruition. I have found the power I need to bring my demon into this world and host him within my body." All four of the figures stirred and one spoke in a deep hollow voice.

"How is this so master? Does the Blood Moon Cycle finally come." A look of annoyance crossed the priest's features.

"No, the Balance Mage was right. I am unable, through any means, to predict the Blood Moon Cycle. But I have found another way through which I might gain the power necessary."

Another of the figure's spoke, this one with a coarse, rasping whisper.

"What is this power you have found master?" The priest waved his hand.

"This information would mean nothing to you. I have called you all here to ask you to perform an important mission. Our greatest threat, the Balance Mage Pravin Solidus is no more. He foolishly sacrificed himself to save the life of a girl ambassador from Hortaal." All four of the figures mumbled and another one spoke, a seedy trill to his otherwise powerful voice.

"This is good news master, nothing can stand in our way now." The others nodded. The priest nodded once.

"You are almost correct, Garynaxiss, but there are still some few who could stand against us. The final three Alenon Mages must be hunted down and destroyed." The four figures' muttering was silenced. The priest smiled twistedly. "Yes, I am sending the four of you to find and kill the Alenon Mages. Together you are powerful enough to destroy them." The first figure to speak spoke again.

"What of Siguard Agamemnon?" The priest harrumphed.

"Unfortunately we will have to wait to deal with him until we have reached our full strength. He is not a fighter, but Agamemnon's barriers are more powerful than any other mage in known history, and he controls the power of the High Temple of Alenon. A place which, for now, we cannot penetrate. He can wait until we are ready to end this world before we finish him. As for the other two, no one knows what tasks they were given to perform, so finding them will be difficult." They all bowed and the one called Garynaxiss spoke.

"We will hunt these mages and tear their essence apart." The priest's twisted smile grew broader.

"Good, go quickly. We cannot afford to have them interfere, we are too close to success to be stopped now." The four figures bowed deeper and turned, leaving through the door that Keliter opened for them. After they had gone and the door had been closed, the high priest spoke again.

"Keliter." Keliter turned and bowed deeply.

"Yes your grace?" The high priest stared at the door for a few moments.

"Once they have left, order all the gates to be shut and sealed. No one leaves this city." A small shock traveled through Keliter.

"Yes your grace, as you command." He turned and left through the door, closing it behind him, and rushed down the hall. He reached the door to the temple and instructed the guards there to bring everyone inside the city and bar the gates. Then he made his way down the steps towards the outer tier of the city, muttering to himself as he went.

"I am sorry, but I think I have come to the end of my service to you, High Priest Borsa. It is time for me to leave Telatia, while I still can."

* * *

Rielle woke with a gasp, jarring Tiasia awake and causing Nysisset to jerk upright. Across the room Vesth was halfway to his feet, hand on his sword and Segine was looking soberly around the room. Rielle took a few moments to collect herself and then sat up.

"I am sorry to wake everyone like that." She apologized. Vesth breathed carefully in relief.

"What was wrong?" Rielle closed her eyes in thought, doing her best to remember the dream she had been having before she woke.

"I had a dream. Something is wrong. I think the Alenon Mages are in danger." Her eyes glazed over as if she were suddenly far away.

"*What did you see?*" Solidus asked her.

"*I am not completely sure. I remember there were six people in a room, all listening to one of them speak. I couldn't understand what he was saying, all I heard was Blood Moon Cycle, and Hunt the Alenon Mages.*" There was a moment of quiet in Rielle's mind before Solidus spoke again.

"*There is no doubt you have the gift. Borsa knows that the only ones capable of stopping his plan are the remaining Alenon Mages. He thinks I am gone so he is sending someone to hunt down and destroy the remaining three. For now Agamemnon is safe. They will not be able to penetrate his barriers until they have reached their full potential strength. But the other two need to be warned. They will sense something, but they will not know the danger until it is too late. Have everyone pack up and leave. Once you reach the bottom of the mountain path, head straight north.*" Rielle nodded and then realized that Tiasia had been tugging at her shoulder. "Rielle? Are you alright?" Rielle shook herself and half smiled at the little girl.

"Yes, I am fine. But we need to leave as soon as we can. We have no time to spare." Vesth and Segine were immediately on their feet and gathering their things.

"Where are we going?" Nysisset asked, seeing no reason to get out of her chair.

"North." Rielle answered. Nysisset rolled her eyes.

"Oh, how very specific of you. I meant, where exactly are we going." Rielle sighed in exasperation as she began to gather her things.

"As resentful as you are being towards me, I see no reason why I should answer you. It doesn't concern you. All you need to know is that Solidus and I are both giving you a direct order to pack up and move out." Nysisset scowled.

"I don't see any reason why I should." Rielle ground her teeth together.

"You can pack now and come willingly, or we will leave what little supplies we have for you here and I will have Sir Segine sling you over his shoulder and carry you down the mountain, your choice. There are more important things that I must attend to, so do not continue to try my patience." Nysisset's scowl was replaced by a look of surprise. This surprise was added to when she looked down to see Tiasia glaring at her angrily. The little girl stuffed an empty pack into Nysisset's arms.

"There is your pack." She said spitefully, sticking her nose in the air and stomping away. Nysisset stared blankly at the pack in her hands and jumped when Solidus appeared beside her and spoke.

"There are travel rations in the cupboard over there." He told her, pointing across the room.

"Master Solidus. You are not speaking through Rielle?" Vesth asked, when he saw the image of Solidus. Solidus shook his head.

"She has to take the time to pack her own things, it would be wrong of me to take control of her right now. And this takes less energy than controlling another person's body. I may need to conserve my strength." Vesth nodded.

"Of course, I understand. So where are we going Master Solidus?" Solidus sighed.

"I thought we had moved past this whole 'Master' business." Vesth quickly looked away and busied himself by tying his bedroll to his pack. Solidus shook his head and spoke again.

"As for where we are going I believe Rielle said north." Vesth finished tying his bedroll and began stuffing the rest of his belongings into the pack.

"North, I understand. What I don't understand is where we are going to the north. There are one, maybe two villages to the north before you run into the Serpent Tongue Mountains. Are we traveling to a village?" Solidus shook his head and Vesth paused.

"Then where?"

"There is the temple." Segine suggested. Solidus nodded. Vesth turned to look at Segine. "What temple?" Segine buckled on his armor as easily as if he were simply putting on a clean tunic.

"The Temple of Fire and Earth is recessed some way into the Serpent Tongue Mountains, nearly due north of here." Solidus nodded.

"There we will find Taeldora Marina, second of the Alenon Mages."

"Second?" Tiasia asked. Solidus smiled down at the small girl.

"Yes little one, by age. I am the oldest and therefore the

first. Marina is the second oldest and Agamemnon is youngest."

"What of the third?" Segine asked. Solidus chuckled.

"You will meet him in time, he will find you, not the other way around. It is balance. I am a Hermit hiding in the mountains, rarely leaving my home to visit the outside world. He is a wanderer, traveling all the world over and over. When the time comes, he will introduce himself. Until then, you must focus on getting to Taeldora Marina."

"What is she doing in the Temple of Fire and Earth?" Rielle asked. Solidus walked to a chair and sat down.

"Fulfilling the task set to her by our Deity. She has been among the monks there for a great many years. It is also a part of the prediction that you all go there." Solidus visibly saddened for a moment and quickly tried to recover, but Rielle had seen.

"What is wrong?" She asked pausing as she finished putting the last few things into her pack. Solidus looked at her and his eyes glistened.

"For now it is nothing. There are secrets I must keep." He glanced around the room, his eyes landing on everyone individually. His eyes lingered on Tiasia for a moment longer and he gave her a smile before looking away again.

"Oh, before I forget, Nysisset." Nysisset harrumphed, but grudgingly looked at Solidus. "It would be best if you hid your tattoos. Most would not question them, but a few would recognize them for what they are and it would give you all away to the demon hosts looking for you." Nysisset scowled.

"But they are my gift from my Deity." Solidus nodded.

"Indeed, but that fact is known, which is why I must ask

you to hide them." Nysisset's scowled deepened, but she nodded reluctantly. She closed her eyes for a moment and her brows drew close together in concentration. Then her black tattoos faded away and were replaced by a small tattoo of a coiled snake on the side of her neck.

"Is that good enough?" She asked spitefully as she opened her eyes again. Solidus nodded.

"Abundantly, thank you." Tiasia, though trying to be angry at Nysisset, could not contain her excitement.

"Wow, neat trick! How did you do it?" Nysisset pointedly ignored the little girl. Tiasia pouted and Solidus chuckled.

"She is a shape shifter, little one. A power given to her through the tattoos she was marked with. She can change any of her personal features if she so desires. She can look like anyone she wants to, provided there is no change in overall size." Vesth slung his full pack over his shoulder.

"That is a very handy trick indeed." Nysisset shrugged indifferently.

"It can be useful, but I prefer my own form." Solidus nodded.

"That is perfectly alright. However, I can see you are all ready to leave. Remember, time is of the essence. Stop in the village near the cliffs only long enough to procure a few extra horses and then continue to the Temple of Fire and Earth. Do not expect to hear much from me during that time. I will give Rielle the instructions you need, everyone listen to her." Once he was sure everyone had agreed, especially Nysisset, he nodded once and then disappeared. Rielle finished tying her pack shut and slung it on her back.

"Let's go. We have a lot of ground to cover." Everyone took

their packs and followed Rielle outside to the horses. The horses were quickly saddled and their riders mounted. Tiasia sat in front of Rielle and Nysisset sat behind Vesth. Segine rode alone with his lance easily held in one hand resting on his knee. They rode down the mountains as quickly as they could safely manage and entered the forest. Tiasia stuck her tongue out at the rotting body of the felle wolf, and Nysisset looked around with great interest.

"I cannot believe I have actually left the mountains." She said. Vesth glanced at her over his shoulder as they rode.

"You are going to see a great many things out here now that you have left. Just wait until you come to the plains, and try not to be too sour to enjoy the view once we get there." Nysisset frowned at Vesth and then went back to admiring her surroundings. It took them about an hour to make it to the village and Vesth and Rielle went in search of horses they could purchase. Tiasia explored around a few buildings and Segine sat proudly atop his mount as a few children came out to excitedly observed the knight.

Nysisset examined her strange new surroundings. The buildings were small and poor, made mostly from logs and mud, and the people went about their business as if there was nothing strange about visitors.

"What is your name?" Asked a small voice. Nysisset searched around and spotted two young children, a boy and a girl, standing beside her. She blinked several times before she realized the question had been directed towards her.

"Nysisset."

"That is a really pretty name." The little girl said, rocking back and forth on the balls of her feet.

"My name is Mindy." Nysisset nodded, unsure of the purpose of the discussion.

"That is... a nice name." She replied. The little girl's face lit up and she excitedly smiled. "You really think so?" Something twisted inside Nysisset and she could feel herself half smiling back.

"That is strange." Came another voice. Nysisset turned to see Tiasia returning from her explorations.

"I didn't think I would ever see you smile." Nysisset frowned and Tiasia pouted. "And now you have ruined it." Just then Rielle and Vesth returned leading two decent looking horses. "Out of the way please little ones." Rielle said, shooing away the gathered children. The little girl beside Nysisset smiled and Nysisset felt the smile tug at the corner of her mouth again before the girl ran off with the others to play.

Wondering what had come over her, Nysisset slid down from Vesth's horse and took the reins from Rielle. She patted the horse's neck and it whinnied and looked back at her with intelligent liquid brown eyes. They stood silently for a moment and then Nysisset turned when she heard a giggle. Vesth had lifted Tiasia up into her saddle and the little girl was laughing and hugging her horse around its neck and playing with its mane and ears. The horse accepted everything patiently and even seemed to enjoy the attention given by the little girl. Vesth adjusted the various straps and the stirrups so that Tiasia could reach and the saddle would fit comfortably around the horse.

"Where did you get these animals?" Nysisset asked.

"They do not seem to be simple domestic creatures." Rielle nodded.

"Indeed. There happened to be a little old traveling salesman in town. He had two trained horses he was trying to peddle off on the people here, but the price he was asking was more than any of them could afford. They looked to be decent mounts and so we bargained to buy them if he would throw in a couple of saddles. He agreed." Nysisset examined the saddle on her horse. "These are well crafted, how did you afford all of this?" Rielle shrugged.

"I am an ambassador from Hortaal and as such have access to a large amount of funds." Then she smiled. "But this time we borrowed the money from Tiasia." Nysisset looked at Tiasia, a little stunned. The little girl giggled and pulled a small handful of sparkling gold coins from one of her pockets. Nysisset was once again shocked.

"More of Lord Khornal's gold?" She asked in surprise. Vesth and Segine chuckled quietly and Rielle smiled as Tiasia stuffed the gold back into her pockets.

"All is well. I am sure if Lord Khornal had been truly upset about losing a few handfuls of gold to a little girl, he would have confronted us before we left this morning." Nysisset nodded sullenly and mounted her horse. They left the village and continued riding through the forest. Nysisset rode beside Tiasia, Rielle and Segine led, and Vesth stayed at the rear to guard their backs. Several times Nysisset found herself looking at Tiasia and thinking about how cute the little girl actually was, then she would catch herself and shake her head to clear it. *Stop being so soft.* She would tell herself. Another hour brought them out onto the rolling plains. Nysisset stared openly at the blank landscape.

"There is nothing." She said. Rielle nodded.

"Very little to look at in these plains. Not like the mountains that hold many countless wonders, the plains have nothing to hold one's interest. However, they do have their own beauty." As if to prove her point, the wind began to blow and the grass bent in golden waves, traveling across the open space in tides the seemed to wash over the ground as far as the eye could see.

"Exquisite." Nysisset muttered.

"Come." Segine said, starting off. "We can reach the next village before nightfall if we ride hard." The others fell in behind the knight and urged their mount's to a ground eating lope. Miles of rolling hills and flat ground swept past as they rode. They made one stop a few hours after midday to quickly eat a small meal and then pressed on. They reached the village just after the sun had set and arranged for a place to stay the night. They woke early the next morning and set off again, this time reaching a village a few miles from the Serpent Tongue mountains a couple hours before sunset. They rested a while and accepted an offer to stay for supper.

"What do you think?" Segine asked after everyone had eaten their fill. "Should we head out again and try for the temple?"

"I think we should stay." Tiasia put forth.

"What do you think we need to do?" Vesth asked Rielle. Rielle shrugged.

"I do not know, I have not heard from Solidus for some time now. Time is very important right now, but I don't know if we should risk trying for the temple. We are awfully close to Telatia and it will be dark in the mountains before it would be out here." Vesth nodded.

"I agree. If we get caught out at night by a horde of those Nibilus creatures, I don't know that we could fight them all off."

"We should stay." Tiasia said again.

"But can we afford to stay here for the night?" Nysisset asked. "It seems to me that the entire reason we have been pushing as hard as we have is because we don't have time to waste." Segine nodded.

"She makes a good point. Do we risk the time, or the Nibilus?"

"We should stay." Tiasia said a third time, happily repeating herself. Rielle sat in thought for a few moments.

"I think we should risk the time. If we get caught off guard by Nibilus, then there will be no one left to warn the mage at the temple. If we are late the mage should be able to defend herself long enough for us to arrive and help, if we leave early tomorrow."

"Agreed." Segine and Vesth both said. Rielle looked to Nysisset, who shrugged.

"I have no opinion."

"But you are a part of our group, you can put forward any suggestions or disagreements you have." Rielle said. They made eye contact for several seconds before Nysisset shrugged again.

"Like I said, I don't have an opinion. What we do doesn't matter as long as we decide to do something." Rielle nodded.

"Very well."

"We should stay." Tiasia repeated again. Rielle smiled down at the little girl.

"Very well. We can stay for tonight and set off in the

morning." The meal was cleaned up and Rielle and Tiasia helped with the dishes while everyone else sat around the table relaxing.

"I could not help but overhear that you were spending the night tonight." Mentioned their host. He was a short little man with no hair and a weathered face and hands. Vesth nodded.

"Yes, we will look into somewhere to stay for the night." The man quickly shook his head.

"Oh that isn't necessary. You may stay in my barn tonight if you wish." Vesth scratched his chin.

"We wouldn't want to impose on your hospitality any more than we already have."

"Oh no, it is no bother at all, truly. It would be an honor to have you spend the night here." Vesth looked to Segine and Nysisset. Both shrugged noncommittally. Vesth turned back to the man.

"Then we would be honored to accept your hospitality once again. But please, let us pay you for your kindness." Vesth reached into a pouch at his side and removed two gold coins and slid them across the table.

"Please take this as a token of our appreciation." The man stared at the coins with wonder before taking them and, stumbling over thanks, rushed into the kitchen to show his wife.

"You are far too generous." Nysisset sniffed. Vesth shrugged his shoulders and reclined back in his chair.

"Perhaps so, but generosity can get you a very long ways." Segine stood.

"Yes, it can. But sitting does not. I think I will take a stroll through town." Vesth nodded and also stood.

"I am inclined to join you. I was never one for sitting." Nysisset scoffed.

"Well you two boys go out and play, I am going to stay here and relax. After riding for two days all I want to do is nothing." Segine laughed heartily and rushed out the door when Nysisset flashed him a sinister glare. Vesth smiled.

"You cannot relax and be resentful at the same time. To gain one you have to let go of the other." Nysisset crossed her arms over her chest.

"When I feel like being philosophically told to calm down, I will make sure to come find you." Vesth shrugged and followed Segine out. Nysisset scowled and stared at the empty table. "Maybe you would feel better sitting outside." Tiasia suggested, wiping her soapy hands on the front of her tunic.

"Don't you have someone else to bother?" Nysisset asked moodily. Tiasia grinned.

"Sure, but they aren't as much fun to talk to." Nysisset sighed.

"Why don't you go steal something then?" Tiasia traced a circle on the ground with her foot.

"Stealing is wrong, and miss Rielle already slapped my wrist for sticking a spoon in my pocket after I had washed it." Nysisset felt herself smirk at this. She made sure she had a straight face and then stood and made her way towards the door.

"Maybe I should go outside, if only to get away from you." She said. Tiasia grinned happily at her as she went and then turned and went back into the kitchen. Nysisset shook her head.

"I don't know why that girl gets to me." She muttered as she closed the door behind her. Tiasia peaked around the corner at the door.

"It's because I'm sneaky and so darn cute." She told the door. With a giggle she turned and made her way back to the basin to help Rielle finish the dishes.

17

Chapter Sixteen

Tiasia sat up and rubbed her eyes. Looking around, she could tell that everyone was sound asleep in their various places around the barn. She considered the possibility of going back to sleep, but decided it would not be worth the effort. She stood and made her way to the door, being careful not to step on Rielle who was sleeping beside her. She slipped out as quietly as she could and began walking around the streets.

"As long as I stay around the barn it should be ok." She whispered to herself. She wandered from house to house, peering in through the windows to see if she could see anyone. The night air was cool and there was a breeze that made Tiasia shiver and pull her small cloak tighter around her. Everything was quiet and Tiasia soon found herself bored and seeking the warmth of her bed. It took her some time to find, but eventually she found her way to the barn again. She headed towards the door and reached out to open it when she heard a small noise. She turned to find a tall, dark figure in a black cloak standing beside the nearest house.

"Hello." Tiasia greeted this new person. The figure did not respond.

"I am Tiasia, what is your name?" Again the figure did not respond. Tiasia took a few steps closer.

"What are you doing out so late? Couldn't you sleep?" The figure's hood tilted, as if nodding. Tiasia frowned.

"I can't sleep either." Then her face lit up with a smile.

"Maybe we can play a game until we are tired." There was a moment or two of silence and then the figure's hood tilted once more.

"Perhaps." Came the seedy reply.

* * *

Rielle jerked awake, pain burning in the center of her back.

"*Fool!*" Solidus cursed. "*Borsa has broken through to the chaos and brought his demon into this world.*" Rielle could see, all too clearly, the dream she had been having the moment before she woke.

"Tiasia is in danger." She whispered urgently. Everything was silent for a moment and then Solidus spoke again, incredible sadness in his voice.

"*It is too late to help her... I am so sorry Rielle.*" Rielle jumped to her feet, immediately noticing the empty bedroll beside her.

"Tiasia!" She screamed. Everyone jerked awake, Vesth rolling to his feet, sword drawn. An agonized scream tore through the night air outside.

"No!" Rielle's voice tearing in her throat as she turned

and burst through the barn door, nearly knocking it from its hinges. Vesth was not far behind and the others were behind them almost as quickly. Rielle froze outside the door, her breath catching in her throat and tears filling her eyes. Thirty feet away stood a figure in black, four writhing tendrils of darkness flowing from its back. At its feet lay a small, lifeless bundle. Anger filled Rielle and she urged her inner power to beat faster, but suddenly it felt as if an icy hand reached out and clutched her center, stopping it's flow.

"You cannot fight him, Rielle. He would kill you." Solidus told her. Rielle struggled against him, squeezing her eyes shut as her tears ran down her face.

"Let me go! I swore I would protect her!" She screamed inwardly.

"She is already gone, Rielle. Her life force has left her. But she wouldn't want you to get yourself killed for no reason while you still have so much to do in this realm." The figure spoke, a powerful voice, marred only by a slight, seedy trill.

"I came searching only the Mage of Alenon said to dwell in the Temple of Fire and Earth. Think of the joy I felt when I also happened to find the group gathering under the final instruction of the Silver Mage. Destroying you, and the Mage at the temple, will bring me great honor and respect." Vesth saw Rielle's inner struggle and stepped forward.

"And what kind of filth are you? To think you could even hope to kill a mage of Alenon is almost blasphemous." A raspy chuckle seemed to echo in the empty air.

"Captain Vesth of Gentry I presume? I am aware you saw what Silver Mage Solidus achieved at the Great Northern Gate. I am sorry to say, however, that the other Alenon Mages are not near so powerful as he. They will all succumb to the power of chaos."

"Shut your mouth, pig." Nysisset growled, her snake tattoo beginning to shimmer. "You are nothing more than a pool of slime. So weak that you can only succeed in killing innocent children. Even the evil that courses through my veins is not so presumptuous." The figure shook his head.

"Tsk tsk tsk, name calling is not necessary. She was simply in my way first. I do say that her essence will be very sweet when I devour it."

"Never." Nysisset spat. "I will send her essence to the heaven realm, Or to be with Great Khornal. I will not let the likes of you have it." She growled again and the snake tattoo on her neck faded and the tattoos around her eyes returned.

"Oh, well, isn't that interesting. The Deity of Evil has sent one of his little Chosen to fight for the Silver Mage. When did Master Solidus convert to the ways of evil I wonder."

"Shut up!" Rielle shouted. "Solidus was a Balance Mage and even the Deity of Evil needs balance." The figure chuckled again.

"You have fire in you, Rielle of Hortaal, I am surprised you haven't tried your meager powers on me yet. What is it that holds you back? Is it fear?" Rielle struggled harder.

"*Please let me fight him.*" She begged.

"*No.*" Came her reply. "*I will deal with this one myself.*" Rielle ceased to struggle.

"*But Master Solidus, that would reveal to everyone that you are still alive.*" Rielle felt Solidus nod.

"*Perhaps, but with Borsa already having torn his demon from the Chaos, the time for secrecy has come to an end."* Rielle nodded and straightened.

"I would know your name before you are destroyed, demon host." The chuckling became insane laughter.

"Destroyed? You are a funny little girl, aren't you? How do you think you will destroy me?" Segine growled and took a step forward, sword poised to strike, but Rielle held out one arm and stopped him.

"Your name demon host." The figure's laughter dropped once again to a self-important chuckle.

"Nothing of my host remains. Over time I have devoured his essence until nothing remained. This body is entirely mine. You may call me Garynaxiss." Rielle nodded once and then her eyes turned silver and Solidus spoke, his powerful voice erasing Rielle's.

"Garynaxiss, to destroy one's host is dangerous, even for a demon." The figure called Garynaxiss flinched back.

"It cannot be." Rielle/Solidus remained expressionless.

"What cannot be? I cannot be? I am surprised to hear such foolishness." Garynaxiss cried out.

"But you are dead! Destroyed by the spell that saved the worthless girl's life." Vesth growled.

"Be still, Vesth." Solidus commanded. Vesth gripped his sword tighter but stepped back a pace.

"My body was destroyed, taken to heal the Girl, but my mind is still intact. I live, using Rielle as my host." Garynaxiss recovered from his earlier outbursts.

"So you have a host now? Well this is most fortuitous then. You could not hope to use even a fraction of your power inside a weak human body such as hers. I can still simply destroy all of you and perhaps my master will raise me in status and place me in control of all his hordes." Rielle/Solidus frowned angrily and lightning played across Solidus's eyes.

"Your lack of concern annoys me." Garynaxiss laughed, though nervously and not as insanely as he had before.

"Should I be concerned? All the legends say that you are one of the most gifted mages ever born, but despite all your power, all your knowledge, all your foresight, you could not even see the death of this young girl, or prevent it." Garynaxiss kicked at Tiasia's lifeless body. Solidus growled. Lightning flashed from Solidus's eyes and the air around Rielle's body rippled and grew heavy with his power.

"I have seen her death since before she was born, and I could have stopped it, but it was forbidden to me. However," Solidus lifted a single hand and placed Rielle's thumb and middle finger together. Garynaxiss, crouched low, ready for an attack.

"What I *am* permitted to do... is remove the abomination that killed her." Solidus snapped his finger, and Garynaxiss simply disappeared. The power in the air disappeared with an earth-shattering crack that shook the ground, rattled the windows in nearby houses, and made the air burn and feel as if it would pull them all apart. Rielle/Solidus stood straight.

"Travel as quickly as you can to the Temple. Nysisset will need the altar there to guide Tiasia's soul to the heaven realm." Segine half bowed and entered the barn to gather the horses. Nysisset took a few steps towards Rielle.

"What did you do to him? Has he been returned to the chaos?" Solidus looked to Nysisset; anger, regret, and painful sorrow all showing plainly on his face.

"Garynaxiss... has ceased to exist." Nysisset gasped in shock and Vesth froze with his sword half way into its scabbard.

"It is forbidden." Nysisset whispered, a terrified break in her voice. Rielle/Solidus nodded.

"Yes, it is. To remove someone's very essence from existence is a severe infraction of magical law, but I will be forgiven for acting in a moment of righteous anger...eventually." Rielle's eyes closed.

"I used a great deal of power and must rest. Rielle will also be very tired as I pushed her body nearly to its breaking point. Take care of her." Rielle's eyes opened and they changed back to their normal bright blue. She blinked a few times and then fell forward. Nysisset stepped forward and caught her, Vesth also reaching out to make sure she did not fall. They stood silently for a moment and then Rielle began to sob quietly into Nysisset's shoulder.

"Tiasia. She is gone." She cried. Nysisset stood awkwardly for a moment and then wrapped her arms around Rielle.

"I know. But I will guide her to a place where she can be safe and... happy." Rielle continued to cry and Nysisset held her until Segine returned with the horses. Vesth placed a hand on Rielle's shoulder. She looked up into his eyes and saw unshed tears held deep inside him.

"We must go. We need to get to the temple as quickly as possible, but we need your light. Will you guide us so that we may help Tiasia find rest?" Rielle sniffed and wiped at her eyes.

"Of course, it is the least I can do." Vesth nodded and then helped her into her saddle. Segine carefully lifted Tiasia's body and carried it back to the horses. Nysisset lifted herself into her saddle and motioned to Segine.

"I will carry her, knight. I will protect her from the demons." Segine nodded and gingerly lifted her into Nysisset's arms. Vesth nodded and turned to Segine, assuming the air of a captain. "Segine, you ride in front with your lance and I will bring up the rear. Nysisset and Rielle will ride between us and Rielle will provide us with light. Be ready at all times and we will reach the temple no matter how many creatures we must fight through to do it." Vesth committed. Segine nodded once and they both leapt into their saddles. Their trek into the mountain was nothing but a blur to any of them. Rielle, using all of her anger and sadness, created a brilliantly shining ball of light that encircled them all. They raced across the few miles of flatlands and into a narrow pass up the mountainside.

The entire way they could hear growls and snarls and yelps of pain, but nothing would venture closer than Rielle's circle of light. No one knew how long it had been when the first sight of the temple came into view. Fires were lit all around it in cauldrons and torches. The massive stone structure looked to be a part of the mountain itself. As they neared the doors Rielle let her light fade away and fell forward in her saddle. Vesth hurried to catch up and placed a steadying hand on her back to prevent her from tumbling out of the saddle. The doors to the temple opened and a white haired woman in a white robe smeared with ash rushed out.

"Please let us enter the temple." Segine spoke, sliding down from his saddle.

"Of course you may enter. I felt Solidus nearby less than an hour ago."

"Mistress Marina?" Rielle groaned from her saddle. The woman ran up to Rielle and slid her out of her saddle and carefully set her on the ground.

"Please," Rielle begged weakly. "Nysisset has to get to the altar."

Marina looked up at Nysisset and nodded.

"You may pass, dark angel, the monks inside will lead you to the altar you seek." Nysisset nodded once and slid carefully from her saddle and carried Tiasia into the temple. Vesth dropped down from his own horse and rushed to Rielle's side.

"Rest now, young one." Marina said, brushing her hand across Rielle's face to force her eyes to close.

"Will she be alright?" Vesth asked. Marina looked at Vesth and then back to Rielle.

"She is burned out, seared by the power forced through her. All of her energy is gone and Solidus is in remission. Help me carry her inside and I will see what can be done." Vesth nodded and maneuvered himself under one of Rielle's arms and lifted her up.

"Sir knight, get your horses inside the temple as quickly as possible. We must get indoors while we can." Segine gathered all the reigns in one hand.

"What do you mean, 'while we can'?" Marina turned and pointed to the sky in the east. "The Blood Moon Cycle begins." Vesth and Segine both turned and watched in awe and horror as a nearly full, blood red moon rose into the sky, turning everything outside a menacing crimson. As the light washed over them, Vesth suddenly felt as if he had been sickened by something tainted.

"Quickly now, inside." Marina urged. "And watch your step, with the light of the moon on you even a minor injury could prove crippling or fatal." They both nodded and hurried inside. The temple doors were quickly pushed shut and barred behind them.

"What should we do now?" Segine asked quietly. Marina directed a few of the monks to take Rielle to a room.

"Now?" She asked, and Segine nodded. Marina sighed. "Now you must rest while the angel and I do our work. Nothing can be decided until the Blood Moon passes. But even then, your journey is far from done. We can only hope now."

"Hope?" Vesth asked. Marina nodded and began to follow the monks who had taken Rielle.

"Hope and pray. Hope and pray that it is not the beginning of the end."

The End
To be continued in book two of
The Moon Cycle: Cycles of Balance